Belios

Belios

Órfhlaith Foyle

THE LILLIPUT PRESS
DUBLIN

First published 2005 by
THE LILLIPUT PRESS
62–63 Sitric Road, Arbour Hill,
Dublin 7, Ireland
www.lilliputpress.ie

A CIP record for this title is available from
The British Library.

1 3 5 7 9 10 8 6 4 2

ISBN 1 84351 067 7

The Lilliput Press receives financial assistance from
An Chomhairle Ealaíon / The Arts Council of Ireland.

Set in 11.5 on 13.5 Perpetua
Printed by MPG Books, Bodmin, Cornwall

For my mother, my father and Joe P.

Belios

PROLOGUE

M Y PSYCHIATRIST LIED TO ME. I wasn't normal. Jesus—if I ever was. I practically lived by kowtowing to the glamorous and the rich shits. The slinky, shiny bitches of both sexes who bared their teeth for a camera lens and availed of me, the pre-eminent glossy, ghost biographer.

I wanted my psychiatrist to shut up. I wanted to rape her. Slam her against her precious thirteenth-century Chinese cupboard and feel her hips shiver and then buck. Sensitivity to shivering has always been important to me. Ram her silent. Wipe out her lies. I wasn't normal.

Sometimes I imagine going back to her, telling her my story, only this time making it different. This time I'd add everything in and keep paying her until the last sentence. Then what, I'd say. What am I now? And perhaps she'd see. Perhaps she'd say, Holy Fuck, haven't you had the life. Not that she would. She likes being solemn and judicious. She'd mention Serotonin and the necessity of pill-dosage.

She'd also ask if I ever kept a diary. I did not. She'd expect self-acceptance on my part and I'd have to disagree. Claire, I'd tell her, it's all shit and it'll keep on being shit. Anyway, you've got it wrong. It's what you can live with that matters. That's what makes you.

If she's interested, I'll explain more. I'll say: Ever make a promise? Ever do a deal? Ever expect God to reply? She's hardly religious and would probably laugh but I hope she'd be curious. So I'd have to tell her why I am as I am now. And it isn't normal.

1

Two things made me agree to William Belios' invitation: Karen was bored and I had refused to dye my hair. That slowly pissed her off. She lay in our bed as I searched for my clothes, then raised her leg and patted her inner thigh—her courtesan call.

I glanced across. 'Get up.'

She smiled. 'Uh no. I'm being disobedient, remember?'

I pulled on my trousers and noticed my hands were shaking. Usually I could have fobbed it off, blamed it on the drink, but it was worse than that. The coming week stretched like an inviting hell and Karen was determined to come.

I looked at her. She was messed up, naked and in daylight her body showed itself for what it was, rarely sexy—a near child-like height and bony limbs. She scowled over at me.

'Can't we mix things up?' she said.

I grabbed my mobile and dialled.

'For fuck's sake, Noah!'

I held up a finger as my call was answered but Karen sat up and kept complaining.

'I only want variation, Noah. It'd be nice if things weren't so safe … if we had something else to occupy us …'

The voice on the other end of the call was deep and female. It kept asking who was calling and, when I couldn't answer, hung up.

'We're never safe,' I said aloud.

'You'd like to think, wouldn't you?' Karen said. 'Hey, I'm into pain. It's great when you do it. It's luscious when I do it. But it's all so regimental and let's face it … it's a bit selfish.'

'Selfish? What? You want company as well?'

'Not that sort. Forget it … who were you ringing? Jerry?'

'William Belios.'

'Did he answer?'

'Someone did. I hung up.'

'For me?'

'Yeah.'

Karen stood on the bed, yawned and then did a ballet jump to the floor. She reached for yesterday's clothes and made her way to the bathroom. At the doorway, she stopped and looked back at me.

'You'll have to look good. Get rid of the grey hair. It makes you look old.'

'I like it.'

'Don't be weird, Noah.' From the bathroom, she shouted, 'Who is this guy? Is he famous?'

I ignored her and re-dialled the number. The phone rang four times before it was answered.

'Yes?' Same deep, female voice.

'What's he famous for?' Karen yelled over running water.

'William Belios,' I said into the phone.

'He isn't here.'

'It's Noah Gilmore,' I explained.

'You. You were supposed to be here.'

'Yeah, I know. Got delayed.'

Karen yelled again. 'Is he some actor I don't know?'

'Who am I talking to?' I asked.

'Medb.'

'One of his daughters?'

'Yes.'

'Well, Medb. I'll be there tonight. I'll be bringing someone. Just put us in the one room. Save on the sheets. Tell William I'm on my way.'

I shut my phone off and joined Karen in the bathroom. Her face was wet and screwed up so I handed her the towel. I nodded at her shoulders.

'Too many bruises?'

She shrugged. 'Better than tattoos.'

She smiled through the mirror and stood on tiptoe to kiss my reflection. It continued to stare back at her—a huge, almost decrepit face. I was supposed to be youngish. That's how gossip magazines described me: a youngish celebrity biographer.

Karen kissed me for real before turning back to the mirror. She had a gentle face, just perfect for ballet heroines. She was always pale with long thin hands. Spinster hands, she called them. I loved things about her. I loved her walk, how it duck-waddled to her toes. I loved her voice when it promised to obey, or when it pretended to cry. I loved her under me.

Karen fixed her mouth with lipstick then glanced at my reflection again.

'When do we head?'

'Now.' I leaned forward to look at myself.

'Jesus, Noah. Dye the fucking grey.'

Halfway from Dublin to Galway, I made Karen drive. I drank my take-away coffee and reread my notes while Karen drove fast through villages and towns. She cursed farmers and animals alike. She despised the West. Her thinking: keep it a museum for the tourists. Every so often she glanced at me.

'All there, huh?' she said.

'As much as I could get,' I replied.

'Is it your usual hatchet job?'

'Fuck off, Karen.'

'Who is he then? I need to know something about him, don't I? Just so I don't look stupid. Is it "William" straightaway? Or "Mr Belios" to begin with?'

'Neither. You won't be talking to him.'

'Fuck, no way, Noah. A whole bloody week in the arsehole of Connacht and I have to be my own company?'

'He's got three children.'

'Brilliant.'

'Older than you.'

'I hope they drink.'

'Hey, was it Pavlova who did it for you?'

'What?'

'Pavlova the swan. Russia. Bolshoi. Ballet.'

'Oh that. God, no. I just wanted to be a princess. Mum said I was light on my feet but too small to be a model. So there it was— ballet. Why?'

I closed my eyes. 'No reason.'

I leaned back as if to sleep but I dug my red file of notes hard against my gut. The pain made me breathe deep. With my eyes shut, I didn't have to see our route closing in on William Belios and in my mind, I felt it all could still be in my imagination. I had never sent letters begging to be seen. The phone call had not happened. The previous, neat invitation had not materialized. 'Mr Gilmore, you may pay a visit.' None of it need actually be part of my life. It need only be Karen and me off for a dirty week in a medieval castle. We would carouse, bite and semi-hate each other as much as we liked, play the primitives in ideal surroundings.

There is no William Belios, I told myself as Karen drove through Galway and out the other side. He never hooked you. But he did. He hooked me when I was ten.

MY MOTHER, Lily, once warned me I was too beautiful. People expect things from beauty, she said. People love you too much. She loved my father. Every morning she'd watch him use his spoon to clean boiled egg from his mouth, then place it back on the saucer, one half of its rim covered in yellow. My father, Tom, was a big man but delicate and usually silent.

I knew the story. Lily ruined her womb in the final attempt to have a child. Four times, Tom had cried when she had promised the next one would be alive. And the next. Until, finally, I arrived. A soft podge of red and blue, nearly dead and Lily told me Tom was afraid to hold me but kept pressing his fingers against my feet, whispering nonsense words at the whole miracle of me. He chose my name and never loved me as much as he loved Lily.

'Isn't he beautiful?' Lily insisted.

Many years later after her death, my father attended my first book launch and stood polite and quiet while I drank and watched him. I saw his large hands pick the pages of my book and his lips move as he read. His hair was wet from the rain outside but he refused to take off his coat.

'You've dressed up,' I joked.

He lifted his gaze. I drank from my glass. Tom had grey eyes and olive skin. I was like him. I had his height and wide face; even our voices were similar. But he was stooping a little and the skin on the back of his hands flaked. He had a heart condition and lived on his own.

He closed the book and replaced it on a pile.

'None of the pictures are yours,' he said.

'No. I decided to write the thing instead.'

'You were supposed to do better, Noah.'

'How about a drink, Dad?'

He said nothing because he didn't have to. Being ashamed of me made him virtuous. I was drinking too much, lived with some dancer and, instead of being a photographer, I wrote piecemeal celebrity shit.

'Just don't have the eye, Dad. You need the eye.'

I looked away to find Karen and I jerked my head for her to come over. She had dressed knowing Tom would show up. Her smile was perfect but at her wrist was a long, dark bruise she had refused to cover up. Tom stared at it. Karen pushed close to my side, then leaned over to tap one fingernail on my book.

'Isn't he marvellous?' she cooed at my father.

Tom now stared at her.

'I like his incisiveness, don't you Daddy-dear?'

'You're drunk,' I said.

'Well, of course I am. Tippety-toes Karen is drunk. But he likes me drunk. We can't manage me any other way, can we, sweetheart?'

She turned to my father. 'Like the dress, Tom?'

My father gave a useless nod.

'Like my feet? I lost my shoes someplace.'

'Karen …' I said.

'Like the bruise your son gave me?' She held up her arm to Tom's face.

I looked at Tom but he refused to look at me. He buttoned his coat and fixed his collar. I watched him search one pocket and then the other for his keys and I said nothing to stop him leaving. Karen put her arms about my waist and nuzzled me. Her teeth nipped a little and then she laughed and swung her head back to look up at my face.

'Fuck the past, darling man. Fuck the whole goddamned past.'

I KNEW VERY LITTLE about William Belios because nothing was known about him beyond a few facts. His wife was dead and buried in Africa. They had three children and after her death he took them back to her family home in Oughterard, Galway, Ireland. There were no books, no interviews. He was non-existent but his photographs remained. Those strange and terrible human faces he caught on lens. Stare at a Belios picture long enough … stare into its eyes and they stare back. They take you in.

When I was ten, I opened a book belonging to Lily and saw a face by William Belios. A Kikuyu tribesman whose skin hung in slack wrinkles beneath his eyes. I pressed my own face close to his, so close I felt the paper on my eyeballs and I imagined how such skin would feel loose and floppy between my fingers.

The Kikuyu man stared at me. He had white nose hairs and was bald. In the left-hand corner of the photograph his hand grasped a stick. His nails were dark with yellow tinges and the skin between his finger and thumb was dry and cracked. I wanted to feel it; put my own fingers into that dry, sharp skin and I knew if I was there, inside that photograph, I would feel as if I was meant to be part of it.

I had my own photographs. Ones Lily took, scrunching her hips low over the ground so her dress got dirty and she ordered me to look, then to smile and then she would kiss me afterwards, saying how beautiful I was, how I was meant for things, maybe to be a famous doctor and rich. Her skirt would swing against me as I tried to walk beside her and keep up with her fairy-tales.

'An astronaut!' I'd say.

'A scientist?' she'd offer.

'A lion-tamer!'

'A deep-sea diver after the sharks?'

'A fireman!'

When I showed her the photograph of the old Kikuyu, she held the book up and away from her face and angled it various ways.

'Isn't it something?' she said and placed it back on the table. She bunched a cleaning cloth in her hand and stretched out her arm to clean the plastic tablecloth. I pulled at the gold cross dangling from her neck to get her attention.

'Will I be like that, Mammy?'

'You're not black, love.' She looked where my fingers pointed to his face. 'Oh, you mean old?'

I shook my head. I couldn't explain but I tried and Lily tried to listen and also keep an eye on the dinner as well as the clock because Tom would be home soon and expect everything ready.

I tried to say what I felt. I tried to describe how I wanted the whole of me inside that photograph, as if I was living there. Lily was getting annoyed but I didn't care. I went over to the bookshelf and took out an album of Lily's photographs and displayed them next to the old man. I wanted her to see.

'What?'

'Don't I look dead, Mammy?'

She slapped me across the face and didn't stop until I was crying hard. 'Mammy, I'm sorry. Mammy, I'll be good.'

There was blood and snot in my mouth and I put my arms over my head to keep it safe until she stopped and then I watched her rip out the page and tear up the old man's face.

'Put the book back,' she said.

'WE'RE HERE,' announced Karen.

I opened my eyes and saw nothing because of the dark. I shut them again to get my bearings, counted a slow five and then opened my eyes. This time I saw a light above a large front door with steps falling into the dark driveway.

'Rich sods,' mumbled Karen as she bent sideways to avoid the steering wheel and strapped on her high heels.

'Yeah,' I said.

Karen straightened up and fixed my tie. She tried to flatten my hair and I saw a ring of dirt on her blouse collar but her make-up was perfect. I had to kiss her. She drew back to study me, her fingers still in my hair.

'You know,' she whispered. 'Let's find a hotel in Galway city. You come out here only when you have to and then come back to me. We'll do things. We can even be tourists.'

I pushed her away and got out of the car. I opened the back door and shoved my red file into my travel bag. I didn't want to look at the house. I undid my tie, coughed and kept coughing until I felt I could breathe.

'Noah,' said Karen.

'What?'

'Someone's at the door.'

I turned and looked. Two people stood at the top of the house steps. Karen waved, came round the back of the car, gave me a filthy look when she noticed my tie and grabbed my hand to drag me forwards onto the steps.

Of the two waiting for us, the girl smiled more. She was not much taller than Karen and neither was the boy beside her. He hung back a little, dressed in a light green suit. He flicked his glances between the girl and me. She had waist-length red hair and wore a purple dress. Her feet were bare and she moved in short tiptoe spurts, introducing herself and her brother.

'Aoife. Jarlath.'

'I thought you were Medb,' I said.

'That's the other one,' said Jarlath.

Aoife took my hand and led me into a large, dim hallway and on to the dining room with a table set for two.

'Where's William?' I said.

'Sleeping,' answered Aoife. 'You can see him tomorrow.'

'We've eaten already,' I lied.

Aoife shrugged and sat on the sofa next to her brother, who handed her a cigarette.

'We smoke too much,' she said.

Karen smiled and sat next to me. 'Noah eats his, don't you, sweetheart?'

I looked around the room. 'I don't see any photographs,' I said.

'None of his,' said Jarlath.

'Right,' I said.

Aoife smiled across. 'Daddy keeps his work separate.' She sat with one leg crossed over the other and leaned forward while she smiled. 'He likes all his stuff close. He has his own part of the house. I suppose everything you want will be there. All the African bits and pieces.'

'A biographer,' said Jarlath.

I looked at Jarlath. Put a dress on him, comb his hair behind his ears and he'd have passed for a girl.

'He has all his notes prepared,' said Karen. 'Your father's in brilliant hands. Have you read anything of Noah's work?'

'Medb says she has,' Jarlath said.

Aoife said, 'She's working. That's why she's not here to greet you.'

'What does she say about my work?' I asked.

Aoife gazed at me for seconds before replying.

'Oh, Medb's hard to please. She's like Daddy that way.'

Later that night Karen insisted on sex. I told her no noise.

'You're scared,' she said afterwards as we lay on the bed. 'Scared about something.'

I said nothing but stared at the ceiling.

'Think I haven't noticed?' she continued. She grabbed my left hand and planted it on her stomach.

'Amn't I real?' she demanded.

'Sure.'

'What do you feel?'

'You.'

'What else?'

'Your skin.'

'What's it like?'

'Like you've been in the gym. Jesus, what do you want me to say?'

'You forget me sometimes, you know. Like tonight. All eyes for those two.'

'They're his children. I need them for the book.'

Karen cuddled her arms about me and pressed her knees against my ribs.

'Promise me something, Noah.'

I kissed her cheek. 'What?'

'As soon as this is over, we'll do other things.'

'Sure,' I said.

'I mean it,' she warned.

'I'm not scared,' I told her.

Karen held my face very close to hers. 'Medb,' she said. 'Ah, made you blink, made you scared.'

'Shut up, Karen.'

Karen mimicked Aoife. ' "Ooh, Medb's like Daddy. She's hard to please." So now, Noah, you're all scared of what she thinks of you. Probably sees right through you.'

I didn't think. I never do. It's the usual excuse and it's always good. I hit Karen straight across the face, grabbed her head and shoved it into the pillow. She made her little yelps and her nails dug into my chest. I shoved my face close to her and she said:

'If you're still scared, I won't scream.'

2

L ATE MORNING the dining-room was empty but the table was set for breakfast. While Karen examined cutlery, I investigated the nearby dresser and the few side-tables, which stood beside two armchairs at the far window. There were piles of magazines underneath a sofa and, propped up between vases of flowers, I found photographs of a young woman smiling at the camera.

'Evelyn,' I said aloud.

'Who?' said Karen.

I held up a photograph for her to see. 'Evelyn. William's wife.'

'Oh right. Nice-looking, I suppose.'

'She's dead.'

'This cutlery is real silver, Noah.'

I put the photograph back. 'Seems a bit weird,' I said. 'Just her photographs.'

Karen had moved from the table and was staring at a painting.

'Jack B. Yeats,' I pointed out.

'Real or print?'

'Print.'

'I like the one of the girl in the red dress. Is that his as well?'

'No idea,' I said.

I shivered a little and then I noticed a patio door open to the cool May morning. I walked out onto the stone veranda that looked onto a vast, near wild garden. Behind me Karen said:

'Bit Anglo-Irish, aren't they? It'd all look brilliant on RTÉ. I bet they even dance at wakes.'

She pulled at my grey hair and tried to kiss me and I grabbed her fingers and held onto them. We stared at each other.

'What?' she said.

'This is what I want, isn't it?' I despised myself for asking but I thought how normal she was, how easily a part of me she was and that me waiting to see a strange recluse was only another day in our lives. We'd drink in some pub tonight and I'd listen to her talk, tear shreds off the weird family we had landed among and even the sex would be the same.

Karen kissed me and ordered me not to worry.

I sat on the patio steps and smoked while I waited. Karen decided to spend the morning exploring Oughterard. She said she'd bring me back a keepsake, something Irish and country-like to look good on the mantlepiece in Dublin. She was glad to be gone out of the place and said she wouldn't be back for ages.

I sat smoking well into late morning. Yeah, I told myself. I had engineered the whole thing. Woke up one morning to my grey hair and large face and decided there was nothing inside me.

'I'm empty,' I had said to Claire, my psychiatrist. 'I think I need my dreams looked at.'

'If you need a dream analyst, I'll tell you,' she said.

She wanted me to do something positive and so I told her there was a man I wanted to meet. I was careful about this. Just a friend from the past who became a photographer.

Claire said: 'You've everything inside you. All the people you've known. All they have said. You couldn't be empty. That's a psychological fact.'

'Jesus, I'm cured,' I said.

Claire was sure I was doing well and decided my medication was just fine. She told me I was normal, getting better and I needn't be back for another three months.

'How fucked up do I have to be to come back sooner?'

Claire pushed back her glasses and tucked her hair behind her ears.

'Look, you're not a serial killer. You're depressed and feel lost. Techniques can help you, you know. If you're spiritual, you can pray.'

'Holy fuck,' I said.

'It's all very normal, really,' she said.

After that last session, I searched for William Belios with a vengeance. There was nothing new on the Internet but a history I more or less had off by heart; his odd background as a missionary priest with the Holy Ghost Fathers, a piece about a later wife and family and samples of his photography. The most infamous story linked with Belios was the unsolved strangulation of his wife. Her children had found her body. Someone later wrote a story about it, using police records as well as speculating on different rumours.

'Ordinary murder,' stated Michael Sullivan, one-time photographic agent to Belios. 'At least that's how people looked at it. The Mau Mau was years gone so there was no point in blaming it. It was later accepted that she was just unlucky. Someone slipped inside the courtyard gate, found her alone, thought she might have money on her and killed her for it.'

'Never found anyone for it?' I asked.

Sullivan shook his bald head and gestured that I help him with a box. We hefted it onto a table and using a knife, he split open the Sellotape binding.

'Belios never did tell me how he felt. I tried to do the usual thing and said I was here if he wanted to talk. I was hoping he wouldn't take me up on it. How do you comfort a man who's lost someone in that fashion? She was quite beautiful. A writer of sorts.'

'Why do you keep his work packed away?'

'Out of fashion, Mr Gilmore. It's a sad fact.' He arranged a group of photographs in a perfect square and invited me to look. 'This one', he pointed, 'is a Dinka tribesman. This one is Masai at some ferry … which one … I thought it was written on the back … ah well, no matter, it is a Masai, the important thing is that the label is correct.'

'This one?' I pointed at a gunman with straps of bullets wrapped round his neck and down to his belt. He was grinning for the camera. There was sweat on his face and an old wound on his left forearm. He had rings across his fingers and wore an army-type uniform with a red-check shirt entwined with the bullet belt.

'ZAPU freedom fighter, circa 1970s on the banks of the Zambezi River,' Sullivan read. 'Belios got around. I used to worry for his life, sometimes. Nothing fazed him. The photographs could be a bit unnerving at times.'

'Really?' I picked up another.

'Hmm, yes. Ah, that one. From the Niger. A nomadic bride to be. Tuareg. The red marks on her face, beauty marks from a powder, called *ekawel*. So it says here. William Belios was very organized with his titles. Can never fault him on that.'

'Always Africa?' I asked.

'Never anywhere else.'

'Must have loved the romance,' I said.

Sullivan began to collect the photographs into a pile. 'I had plans to make him more amenable to public interest. Attend gallery openings. Do a few interviews. Invest some time in normal public relations, but he wasn't interested. I met his wife. I met his children. I wasn't particularly interested in them. They kept to themselves.

'No, I would never believe William Belios to be a romantic. He was … organized. He was methodical. Always could find a face. He knew how to photograph faces. And you, Mr Gilmore … I can't say I know your work.'

'Writer, mostly. I dabble a bit in photography.'

'Do you?' smiled Sullivan.

'I'm interested in Belios' story.'

'Are you?'

'I'd like to contact him, Mr Sullivan.'

He nodded his head and began to put Belios' photographs back into the box. He pressed it closed.

I smiled and made myself look friendly. 'Listen, Mr Sullivan. The man's a fucking genius. We need his type these days. Look what we're fed most of the time. Shit masquerading as art. Literally. Photographic exhibitions designed to make the photographer look good.

Public relations gone mad—that's what art is now. No wonder William Belios has made himself scarce.'

Sullivan went over to his desk and sat on a red leather chair. I recognized a negotiation move and so I dawdled at the box just long enough for him to notice. Hunger looks good when you use it well. My hands threatened to shake so I dug one into my pocket and willed the other as still as I could make it.

Sullivan watched me as I sat opposite him.

'Please don't tell me he's dead,' I said.

'No, but he's dying. He's dying quite fast. Probably won't see out the summer.'

'Christ.'

'Cancer, I believe.'

'So you still talk with him?'

'I have contact with his daughter, mainly. She's the artist in the family now. Quite unlike him but couldn't be anything else other than a continuation. A walking paradox with paints and pencil, that girl.'

Sullivan was a bit of a find and he was no fucking fool. He knew about me. Probably despised me deep down but he also knew how to be polite and, no doubt, he was curious.

Photographs in a box. How the fuck does that happen? My work ends up in recycling bins but at least it's shit.

'Really?' Claire had said at one session. 'Is that how you see your contribution to society?'

'Absolutely, Claire. Recycled shit.'

Sullivan leaned forward and smiled just a little as he fiddled with his fountain pen.

'The reality is, Mr Gilmore … is that William Belios is an adamant recluse. He doesn't see anybody. He has his family and of course he has his memories and now and again, someone like you comes along; perhaps you're an admirer, or perhaps you have different ideas and with your track record as a writer, I'd be rather averse to allowing you to contact him.'

'So he can be contacted, Mr Sullivan?'

'Mr Gilmore …'

'Mr Sullivan …' I stood up and shoved my chair closer to the desk. He straightened up. Negotiation time. I smiled as much as my face would move and I leaned forward. I saw a small notebook close to Sullivan's hand and so I played for all I was worth.

'Mr Sullivan. I understand your trepidation. I have the same problem. I can't tell you how often I've been approached with similar requests. I've a sixth sense where they're concerned. I just put it down to the dark side of the job. However ... and this is rare, Mr Sullivan ... I believe that there are some people in this world who need to be known and William Belios is one of them.'

I played my trump card and produced the photograph of William Belios. I let it fall to the desk right under his gaze.

'That's him, isn't it? Maybe round the same time as you knew him? You didn't by any chance take the photo, did you, Mr Sullivan?' I knew damn well that he hadn't but no harm in playing the innocent.

Sullivan shook his head as he picked up the photograph.

'Like gold dust,' I said. 'Found it in some junk collection in a buy-and-sell market for hard-up photographers. There was an article with it—more a story really. It mentioned his wife and kids. It also mentioned his wife's murder. This guy, the guy who wrote it ... Stephen ...'

'Stephen Bankes.'

'Know him, Mr Sullivan?'

'Amateur photographer. Ended up in Australia and became an estate agent. He wasn't much with a camera to begin with. Hadn't any eye, as they say. He visited Belios, then came back and dug out a little fame for himself with this photograph. I read the article but it was too gushing for my taste. Relied too much on rumours and I suspect he fantasized about "white mischief" in Africa.'

I was sweating. My fingers hooked along the leaf-and-berries design along the rim of Sullivan's desk. I knew I had to stay calm. I knew my smile had to seem perfect. I knew everything I was to say had to mean something to this old man.

'You hide his work in boxes, Mr Sullivan. He hardly exists anymore and what is allowed to take his place? Recycled shit ... I mean that's what we've reduced art to. I want people to know Belios. I want people to see the man who caught such faces on film. I want people to realize what drove him to live in another country, photograph the people he found there and then disappear. Nothing heard of him since.'

I knew I sounded good—just the right side of passionate admiration with a touch of evangelical zeal. Hardly anyone can resist that. Not the people I know. Not even proper Mr Sullivan, whose fingers fiddled again with his pen, then picked it up when it fell on the notebook. He didn't move his hand away but he shook his head.

I panicked. I shoved one hand into my pocket and took out my card—the classic way of looking normal when things weren't going to plan. What do I do when the subject refuses to put out? Smile like I mean it and present them with my card and begin my spiel.

'Mr Sullivan ... be assured I am a professional and ...'

He held up his pen, smiled and then wrote out something on his notebook, tore off the page and handed it to me.

'It's his home address. Well, originally, it was Evelyn's family home. He lives there now. His children are caring for him. If he doesn't reply, Mr Gilmore, well ... that's really no concern of mine.'

For just over two months, William Belios ignored my letters until an invitation was sent back, 'You may pay a visit.'

I almost destroyed the invitation because my reflection ridiculed me. Thick, pouchy flesh and hardly my mother's beauty anymore. William Belios would see underneath the lie, see a cut-price ghostwriter with useless dreams.

'NOAH GILMORE,' said a voice.

A girl, a woman, stood to my far right on the bottom patio step. She was taller than Aoife and her waist had a doll-like look. She wore a blue long-sleeved blouse and her skirt fell to above her ankles. Her hair was gathered up, but messy. There was dirt on her face and she carried a garden trowel in one hand, the guts of a plant in the other.

'Medb, right?'

I liked her stance. One hip jutted against the stone balustrade. I liked her face. It was clear, young and pissed off.

'The acolyte,' she said.

'Biographer, actually.'

I remained where I was but offered her a cigarette. She shook her head and rubbed her face with the hand that held the trowel.

'Hard work,' I remarked.

She glanced at me, then shifted stance and banged the trowel against the stone to loosen the dirt.

'You're the gardener,' I said.

'Sometimes.' She used her fingers to scrape the remaining clay off the trowel.

'Mad garden,' I complimented. 'Full of wild things—like in a storybook?'

'Depends.' She dropped the trowel, dropped the plants and slapped her hands clean, then picked up the plants again.

I inhaled, then blew out. 'You don't want me here, do you?'

'You're not necessary,' she answered and looked me straight in the eye.

I stared back. I've often liked people who scare me. Mostly because it's show, nothing more than an easy snarl I can describe in their biography, some toughness to them I can play up to, yet watching Medb made me cold and made me sweat. I rubbed my neck and began a mantra in my head. Come closer. Come closer. The bitch with the waist. Come closer. Saliva was making my cigarette wet and I stubbed it out. Come closer, I willed her. The bitch with the dead plants. Come closer.

I saw her waist, the band of her skirt, and wondered how she would feel there, how narrow her flesh and bones—as if between my fingers—I could tear her open.

'Your father invited me,' I said.

She blew out against a bit of hair that stuck along her mouth. Then she said: 'Show me the photograph.'

I took it from my pocket and handed it to her. She cupped it in both hands, then turned it over.

'Nothing written on the back,' I said. 'But I got it corroborated. Michael Sullivan recognized him straight away. It is him, isn't it, Medb?'

She handed it back. 'Where?'

'In a book, magazine someplace. Can't exactly remember.'

I lit another cigarette while I half-watched her and the garden. There was clay on her skirt and she wore wellington boots. I looked over at the garden, complete with the odd flowerbed here and there. There was a path leading towards the back where an oak tree hulked over a collection of terracotta pots, some with plants, some empty.

I glanced up at Medb, ready with a smile, but she stopped me just by her look, her very calm, pink-with-sweat face and I wanted to touch her. I wanted to lay my palm against the doll-like waist and smash her fist free of those dead plants.

I stood up, ready for some truce, and she retreated one step. I held up her father's photograph more for her gaze than mine.

'Strange thing to say,' I said. 'Me not being necessary. You're father wants to talk. I want to listen.' I put the photograph back inside my pocket. 'It'd be great if you could help; make sure I don't get dates wrong, spell names right—that sort of thing.'

Her right boot poked my cigarette butts off the final stone step and squashed them into the ground.

'Mr Gilmore,' she said and swung sideways from my gaze, then paused in climbing the steps to the patio above.

I looked up after her. 'Yes?'

She jabbed an index finger in the air. 'Join the dots.'

When she reached the patio, she turned and said, 'You'll manage that, won't you? Oh, hi Aoife,' she greeted her sister, who rushed out through the patio door, glanced at Medb and then called to me.

'Daddy will see you now.'

I came up the stairs, aware of Medb as she pulled off her wellingtons.

'Has he kept anything down?' Medb asked Aoife.

'Not yet.' Aoife glanced at me. 'You have to go and see him now.'

Before I followed Aoife, I stepped close to Medb as she bent a little from her waist to brush the drying clay from her skirt. She straightened up when she sensed me nearing. I watched her calm, pink face; saw how blue her eyes were and how they narrowed as I pressed closer.

AOIFE WALKED ACROSS the main hallway, up the staircase and onto the upper landing, glancing back every few steps or so to make sure I was following. She turned left at the far end of the landing and stopped at a door. She smoothed her hair to her shoulders and then studied my suit.

'You stink of smoke.'

'Daddy doesn't like that?' I presumed.

She shrugged. 'Smoking helped to ruin him. At least that's how the doctors have it written down. He doesn't believe them. He says it's just natural. Just God getting him where it hurts.'

'Does he have long?'

'Long enough for you.'

'I can change my suit,' I offered.

'Don't bother. He wants to use up all the time he has left.'

She turned to knock on the door.

'It must be difficult,' I said.

Aoife curled her fingers back into a fist. 'What is?'

'Watching someone die.'

She shrugged. 'It's my job at the moment.'

'What did you do before?'

Aoife looked at me. 'I was married for a few years.' She glanced at the door. 'I was even pregnant but now I'm an ex-wife and nurse-maid.'

'And the others?'

'Jarlath is a teacher but only because he's not going anywhere else and Medb's an artist because she wants to be.'

Her eyes had a sheen of anger but I leaned against the wall so I could look relaxed and harmless.

'And what will you do?'

'I've no idea,' Aoife replied, knocked on the door and wrenched it open. 'Daddy, he's here!'

She motioned me inside and shut the door behind her as she left. I took my time looking. I was in a large room; a huge window overlooking the gardens and the far-off Maam Turks had supplanted the facing wall. The light from the window lit up what was left of William Belios' world. Wood or stone figurines stood on tables;

carved heads were jammed against books; Batik paintings of African scenes hung on the walls; and a large dagger, almost the shape and length of a pirate's cutlass, braced itself under the elephant tusk fastened to the wall above the fireplace. There was cheetah or leopard skin bunched about the sofa cushions and a black and white chess set in a game. I looked for the photographs and saw them mounted on the left-hand wall, framed in various sizes with odd little brass-shaded lamps angled up towards each photographed face.

'Mr Gilmore.'

I turned to my right and saw an old man in an electric wheel-chair, complete with drip and strapped-on oxygen tank.

'It's good of you to come, Mr Gilmore. Sit. Sit over there.'

I sat on the sofa and he rolled up close. His skin glistened in the light and when he shook my hand, his was oily and warm.

'Almond oil,' he smiled at my expression. 'Aoife insists on it. She says it makes me look healthy. Keeps my skin from falling off.'

'You look healthy,' I lied.

'Michael Sullivan warned you I was dying, Mr Gilmore?'

'Yes.'

'So here you are.'

'Yes.'

'All ready to dig out a story.'

I shrugged, smiled and laid my hands palm open. 'It's what I'm good at. I help people tell their stories.'

'How convenient,' he said.

I looked at the stretched skin of his face. He was pale grey and his breath spat out his words.

'I should be dead, Mr Gilmore. That's what you are telling yourself, isn't it?'

'I'm no doctor, Mr Belios.'

'No, of course not, Mr Gilmore, but I always say that death brings the parasites scuttling.'

Belios motioned down the side of his wheelchair and I pulled out a pile of letters.

I recognized each one. All of my letters from the past six months addressed to William Belios and fastened together with an elastic band. I flicked their edges twice before I noticed the scrawl of pen on each one.

William Belios leaned forward and nodded at the first envelope. 'Read.'

'The letter?' I supposed but Belios shook his head and pointed to the red pen marks. I undid the elastic band and read: 'Groupie.' On the second, I read: 'How old?' Another had the words 'Tarzan-Lover.' There were more. 'Pathetic.' A phrase: 'Wants fairy tales.' A question: 'What shit is this?' The final and most recent I had sent had one word: 'Fraud.'

'Medb?' I said

'Her way,' said Belios.

I sat back on the sofa and felt the cheetah skin crumple behind me. Belios was grinning and waiting for my move. His fingers had clawed into the wheelchair's arms and were red with the strain of holding himself straight.

'Well,' I said at last. 'She's trying to protect you.'

'Not her job,' said William Belios.

I tried another angle. 'She's afraid I'll use you.'

'She knows you will, Mr Gilmore.'

I sat forward with fingers touching. I looked the part. I looked professional. I looked as if I could write the whole goddamned Belios saga with my eyes closed and still win the Pulitzer for non-fiction, but first interviews with prospective subjects are dicey experiences. You need to suss what they're hiding from you. Maybe they hate your fucking guts. Maybe they'll actually collude with you. Maybe they prefer to tease you to begin with … hint at their half-open secrets and so you play along.

I smiled and said: 'Of course I'll use you, Mr Belios. I do that best of all.'

Belios' thin wrists gave way and he slumped back into his chair. He held his hand out for the letters and I watched as he stuffed the bundle deep into the side of his chair. That finished, he looked at me.

'Want to know how many have followed me, Mr Gilmore?'

'How many?'

'Too many to remember. All with their little wet dreams about me, with their portfolios all dressed up to impress me. I had them everywhere. I had them in Africa coming off the planes and playing explorer with their one or two phrases learned off by heart. I had them when I travelled, mewling like puppies desperate to be loved.'

'There's nothing wrong with having heroes, Mr Belios.'

'That sounds good,' said Belios. 'Yes, that sounds good.'

I knew what I had written in those letters. I knew how I had crawled to this man and composed each page as if I was in my own movie. I added every trick of pathos. I invented every dream I could. And in my final letter, I put in my memory of the old Kikuyu man.

'You told me to come,' I said.

William Belios held up his hand. 'The last letter was the best.'

'It was the truth,' I said.

He nodded and smiled and his oil-basted skin shone in the window light. He raised his left arm at the photographs on the wall.

'They are all there,' he said.

I stood up and walked over to the wall. My private 'Stations of the Cross' hung in neat batches with their individual lamps. William Belios rolled up close behind me.

'Some hack once called me the "Van Gogh of faces",' he said. 'What would you do if you had such a gift, Mr Gilmore?'

'I'd use it.'

'Exactly.'

'This one?' I pointed out a stone castle.

'Fort of Jesus, Mombasa. A Portuguese stronghold that also held slaves. I think that day, I just liked the shadows people made against the walls.'

'Nice,' I said.

William Belios sat hunched in his chair. I tried to concentrate on the faces on the wall. The little Tuareg nomadic bride was there. A water-carrier from somewhere else with his face turned sideways towards the camera—old but maybe young with three teeth missing. His hands hooked into skin bags distended with water and his head angled back with the force of his smile.

'His name was Christopher,' said Belios. 'One of my first photographs. His parents were slaughtered in the Biafran war in Nigeria.

He was fascinated with America and I told him that in order to survive in America, he would have to find God. So he baptized himself Christopher and became a minister.'

'What happened to him?'

Belios shrugged. 'He may have got out. Who knows?'

I stepped back to level with the wheelchair and thought of my last letter squashed with the others and hidden beside Belios' withered thigh. I had written it drunk while Karen had slept and maybe I had cried but I didn't want to remember and I knew I had written 'please'. I knew I had written how I wanted to be saved from what was inside me. I knew I had written that the old Kikuyu man had never left me. I had written it all as if I was a child, drunk and grizzled with a mad dream to see it all through.

I wanted it back.

Aoife came in, carrying a bowl of something on a tray. She walked across the room at the same time as her father pressed a button and drove his wheelchair to a nearby side-table. The drip swung above his head and Aoife steadied it. She and Belios bent their heads close together over the tray and her hand touched his collarbone, then her fingers spread out along his skin.

His breathing scraped over hers in loud grating spurts. She 'ssh ssh'd' and pressed her lips onto his cheek.

I coughed to remind her I was watching.

Belios looked at me. 'So-called breakfast,' he said. 'Semolina. The doctors say that if I can keep something down and grow fat enough to withstand chemotherapy, I may survive for a little while longer.'

Aoife was now checking the drip. She followed its line from its pouch, through the wheelchair's armrest and up to Belios' arm. He flinched a little as she touched it and she looked at him.

There are certain looks between people. You can gauge them, categorize them, and some are dead easy to recognize since they repeat themselves everywhere you go. Others defy you. Aoife's fingers on her father's skin neither pinched to test the amount of fat he may have gained, nor did they give the sort of touch any daughters' would.

I didn't want to guess. I sat down and breathed through my mouth.

'He admires my photographs, Aoife.'

Aoife glanced over at me. 'They're just people.'

She looked different. Her hair was caught up and pulled tight into a smooth, high hairstyle. She looked older. She looked like her mother. She sat down opposite her father and swirled the semolina with the teaspoon. Belios leaned his head closer as Aoife raised the spoon to his mouth. He sucked a little and his Adam's apple moved up and down while the sound of his staccato breathing filled the room. Bubbles of semolina spurted back onto the spoon.

Belios drew back a little. He sucked in air. 'You don't look comfortable, Mr Gilmore.'

'He is comfortable,' said Aoife. 'He has his girlfriend with him. You have to eat a little.'

'I'd prefer a cigarette,' said Belios. 'It never hurts as much but Aoife forbids it. She loves me, you see.' He leaned his face in again towards the spoon and sucked up some more. Aoife held a tissue underneath to catch any dribbles. Belios pulled back, shook his head and settled back into his wheelchair.

'Aoife looks like her mother,' I said.

I looked at Belios, expecting more, but he had closed his eyes and he seemed to sleep.

Aoife glanced at me. 'Would you like a drink?' She got up and walked over to a small drinks trolley. She poured out two glasses of whiskey and handed one to me.

'Thanks.'

She sat down. Oval face. Red hair. Her mother's eyes. Her mother's hair.

'Does it make him feel good?' I asked and nodded at her hair. 'To have you look like her?'

She sat on the edge of her chair and said: 'He's not asleep. Are you, Daddy?'

'Why do you call him that?'

'Because he likes it.'

'It's unnerving,' I said.

'Unnerving,' said Aoife. 'Unnerving. How is it unnerving?'

'It's the sort of word only a kid should say,' I replied.

I drank again. The room was too bright and Aoife looked too perfect as her mother—as if she made a photograph come alive.

I looked at Belios. His mouth had dropped open and his lips were white with dried semolina. 'You must love him very much, Aoife … to have become a nursemaid.'

Aoife turned her face towards me. She smiled just a little and said, 'Nothing like you would be able to write.'

'I can write about love,' I told her.

I imagined myself outside the room, outside the house and inside some shop with Karen bleating about tourist prices; Karen real and soft beside me; Karen playing at being happy and me playing at being loving.

I imagined how easy it would be to play.

I finished my drink and rolled the glass between my hands.

'Nothing wrong with love,' I said.

Aoife brushed her father's lips with her fingers, stood up and held the tray against her hip while she bent to kiss him before turning to me: 'If he throws up any of it, there are tissues in that box by the window.'

I waited until she closed the door behind her. 'Belios,' I said, but he didn't answer. I stood up and went over to the gallery of photographs.

PHOTOGRAPHY WAS MEANT to save me. That's what I had wanted from the moment I saw the old Kikuyu man. I wanted to hold his face, wanted to be caught like him, wanted to seem that real and if I am to be honest, it began before that. It began with my mother.

Lily adored her face. She had skin that shone in front of the mirror and I loved watching how it could change the way she wanted it to. She had once been a model yet deserted that life when, while holidaying in our village, she decided to buy lamb chops from the local butcher.

Tom Gilmore was a big-faced big-shouldered man with hands as beautiful as hers and he ran his fingers alongside his butcher's coat to get rid of the animal fat in his nails before handing her the chops.

Lily knew what she was doing. She needed a new adventure in her life and liked the look of such a big man with narrow, gentle fingers and eyes that made her shiver. She convinced herself that life could be as different as she longed for it to be. No more drink parties and avoiding family life. No more half-guilty sex while still desiring Communion on Sundays—just a one-road village, one church and three pubs.

Lily never told Tom who she really was and he loved her all the more. He demolished the back wall of his tiny butcher-house and built her a kitchen, as well as another room. He welcomed this new obsession into his life, this brilliant woman who made him do things he had never imagined he could do.

One Christmas I was desperate to hurt him and I asked did he ever see Mam and I as meat too? Ever imagine us as dead hanging meat in his back fridge? He beat me to a pulp then and stuffed his full face into mine so that our eyes saw each other. 'You little bastard fuck. We should never have wanted you.'

Lily never stopped Tom in a rage. She'd shrug as she stared at her own reflection and avoided looking at my bruised face. Her fingers would shake very little as she put on make-up.

'But I wanted you,' she never forgot to say.

I was something beautiful to her. Something like him with her inside. I reminded her of why she chose Tom and his delicate butcher-touch.

'You love him too much,' Tom accused her.

I tried to keep outside their love and when they decided on boarding school for me, I went. I bullied younger boys and at Mass I repeated my own litany of Fuck God. Fuck God. Fuck. Mostly I was despised, left in the back of the class, gouging my name into the corners of wooden desks where no one could find my mark. I liked being ignored. It made me powerful and I began to watch people. Mainly their faces and always at certain moments when their defences were down, when fear or anger shone through, or repulsion or sometimes love. I soon learned that people are always truer when their heart is being used, whether it's love or hate or anything in between. Catch a face then and you have something.

I had my father's face with my mother inside and I was always dead, as if I was somewhere else, rammed neat and innocuous into some corner of my body and forgotten.

Photography taught me that.

Lily was obsessed with her camera. Tom enjoyed the pictures she took of him and slotted his big body into whatever milieu she created. He stood behind the meat counter, at the beach, in a pub or outside the post-office.

She told him he was beautiful, that she loved him and wanted always to be reminded of him. He seemed to live because of her. She taught him how to decorate his meat for display—real parsley instead of the green plastic shit, tomatoes carved open like roses and marinated chicken from China. My father accepted it all until my pictures began to overlap his on the sitting-room wall.

Lily's explanation was easy. She just wanted to see the both of us together. She wanted to be reminded of us both.

When I returned home one year from boarding school almost Tom's height and with his voice, Lily placed her hands on mine and held them to her face. Her skin had hardly changed except for a dryness, like on the skin of a not-so-fresh apple: still beautiful but spoiled. She whispered that she wanted me to stay and my father sat glum in front of the television. He had thickened in that year. His neck was round and soft and he had employed a new man to open the shop in the mornings.

I heard them at night and I could imagine my mother under him, being mashed into the bed. I heard her say, 'I love you. I love you. Don't I always love you?'

I poured myself whiskey on those nights and sat staring at Lily's gallery on the wall and it did nothing for me. I was always dead inside those photographs, no matter how Lily manipulated angles and light and insisted I was beautiful.

While he fucked her upstairs, I fucked myself to myself on that wall, my dead young face with clear skin and just as she liked me.

'OLD, AREN'T YOU?' Belios said after a while.

I stepped back, breathed slow and kept the smile on my face.

'Not really,' I replied. I dragged a chair to sit opposite him. 'I'm thirty-six.' I glanced down at his rug-covered lap and thought of my letters. 'Thirty-six,' I repeated.

'Tell me what you want, Mr Gilmore.'

'I want to write your story. I think it's important you're remembered.'

'Why?'

'Because of the life you've led. Because of what you've done with it. Because of what you have on these walls.'

Belios raised his hand to his face and rubbed his forehead. Dried flakes of skin shed down to his knees and he brushed away those he could reach. 'I'm wasting to death,' he said.

'I'm sorry,' I said.

'Why should you be?' His eyes glanced on the wall of photographs behind me. 'Why should you parrot me your sympathy? Do you think I'm grateful?' He hitched his body sideways in the chair and I saw my letters. 'Take them, Mr Gilmore.'

I took them.

Belios shrugged. 'I like frauds. I've always considered them worthwhile.'

'I'm not a fraud,' I said.

Belios leaned forward. 'Mr Gilmore, you're thirty-six and I've seen what you write. You use verbs only a child can get away with and each exclamation point is timed—da ... da ... da! Look behind you, Mr Gilmore. Look at what I have done in my life. And you think you can translate that into words? You believe you can take what you see in my work and make me famous?'

I held up another envelope. 'Medb thinks I'm a sick groupie?'

'Oh,' said Belios, 'Medb has her ideas. She likes to think things and she expects all of us to listen. I gave her your letters because she always said someone would find me in the end and I wanted her to see the calibre of the hunter. She was hardly impressed ...' Belios nodded at the drinks table. 'Would you like a drink? You'll have to pour.'

39

'So I'm a hunter, am I?' I said.

His head nodded. 'In your line of work, Mr Gilmore, you must hunt people rather well.'

'I write biographies.'

'It's all the same, isn't it? A hunter has his prey; a biographer has his subject.'

I sipped my drink and placed it on the windowsill. 'And Medb wasn't impressed?'

Belios smiled. 'Mr Gilmore, frauds are the most satisfying of people. I admire their desperation.'

'How desperate do you think I am?'

'According to your letters, it is eating you up.'

'They tell you that?'

'Your last one made me decide to invite you.'

I tried to laugh and almost reached for my glass but didn't. Instead, I picked out the last letter, ignored the red pen on the envelope and unfolded the pages.

'The last paragraph,' said Belios.

I didn't read it out but I could hear my drunken plea in my head.

Mr Belios, do you believe in heroes?

I saw my drunken face close to the paper and the drooled-out words as I had written them.

I want to be saved.

Fuck you, I mouthed to myself. I didn't look at Belios. I gathered up the letters and shoved them into my pocket. I stood up. Bile rose from my gut and I drank up the whiskey, held it so that it stung my mouth, made my eyes water and made the vomit go back down.

I don't remember walking towards the door but I stopped not because Belios called me back but because I imagined Medb was waiting on the other side of the door. I could see her face and I realized she didn't look like her father. Her smile had been nothing like his; her waist, her arms, her wellingtons, and I willed her in.

Come close. You doll-like bitch. Come close you shit-woman with your red pen. Come close so I can feel you—all of you behind your blouse and skirt; close about me so that my fists can pull you apart and fit you to every piece of me.

'Mr Gilmore!'

I didn't turn. I had to steady myself first.

'What?' I said.

'I used to be a priest. I used to believe in God. I loved the Church. All that holiness filled me with ecstasy. All that greatness. That absolute glory. It gets into you. It ruins you for anything else and once you have that, humility is shit.'

I turned and faced him. William Belios fastened into his chair with a goblin curve to his spine and his eyes glinted up at me.

'Saving is for fools, Mr Gilmore.'

I ballsed it out. 'That's a fact, is it?'

Belios rested back in his chair. 'But first things first. I would like a cigarette.'

I gave him one. Lit it and lit mine. Belios gulped in the smoke and his face shook with the effort while I returned to the sofa.

Aloud I said: 'We need to devise a schedule.'

'I see,' said Belios.

'Morning, afternoon, dead of night. Whenever you like to talk. I'm instantly adaptable.' I motioned towards his gallery wall. 'I'll need you to decide what photographs you want to use. It's not too early to think of that.' I forced my patter to its professional tone: 'Have to think of structure ... keep us focused. We can use all your favourites ... don't forget the family album.'

Belios said nothing. I lit another cigarette. I could have said more. I could have said: Listen—no one gets to your age without secrets. Give me a few. I'll make them marvellous. I'll make them necessary to the story. I'll make you necessary.

I slouched into the sofa and flicked ash into my palm.

'There is no family album, Mr Gilmore.'

'You lost it?' I prompted.

'No.'

'Thieving fans?'

'No.'

'Moving house?'

'I don't expect you to understand.'

'I could if I really tried,' I promised.

Belios put his cigarette out against the arm of his wheelchair. He looked at me and smiled.

'Life is created through a series of additions, Mr Gilmore. Some additions survive. Most die. My wife died. My children survived. I never photographed ... my family, so I'm afraid you'll have to make do.'

'Why not?'

'Simple reason, really. They were never useful to me.'

I exhaled for effect and said: 'That sounds sinister, Mr Belios.'

Belios nodded. 'But I was never a fraud.'

'Not like me?'

'Not like you.'

I counted to ten—all the more to make him wait. All the more so he sat there with nothing else to unnerve me but his face and its fucked up, glistening smile. I dug my back into the sofa, shook my head and coughed.

'A hunter keeps things close to his chest,' I said. I took out the photograph of a younger Belios and held it up. I angled my head to glance at it. The younger Belios sat in a dark wood chair outside a large stone house. His hand was raised to shade his face from the sun. His eyes couldn't be seen but it was Belios.

I warmed up. I sat up and lusted for some sort of kill. I needed a flourish of victory. Put the sick bastard down. I'm the one with re-useable legs. I'm the one who has a life.

'Tell me about this. Someone took this. The kids or the wife or a nearby camel boy?'

I flicked the photo face down and offered it to Belios. He didn't move. His grey flaking face stared at me and I stared back. I watched him as I had watched others. I knew I had got to him. The light from outside shone up the bones in his face, superimposed his skull over his features and a nerve flicked off-on, off-on at his temple.

Jesus, I needed a camera. Catch his face. Nail it to the wall and I'd genuflect.

'Where did you find it?' said Belios.

'Some magazine.'

'I'd forgotten it,' said Belios.

'You can keep it,' I said but he still didn't move. So I dropped it. I glanced down at it and back up at him. 'Not want to pick it up?'

I got to my feet and walked over to admire the elephant tusk above the fireplace.

'Never been to Africa,' I said. 'I suppose it's not much good to anyone now. People are dying too quickly over there. Aids. War. You must miss it though. Ireland after Africa? Two extremes. Ever photograph people here?'

'No.'

'Too familiar?'

'Too Irish,' Belios replied.

He turned his face and looked at me.

'I prefer to talk in the evening.'

'Suit yourself,' I said. I walked towards the door. 'Watch you don't roll over your photo.'

'Mr Gilmore,' said Belios.

'Yeah?'

'I didn't invite you. Medb did.'

Mr Gilmore—you may pay a visit.

'I told you she has these ideas,' continued Belios. 'She's prepared to watch you make a fool of yourself and I have a little time on my hands.'

KAREN WAS DANCING. It was only when she danced that I remembered how neat and disguised her muscles were. She was performing the 'Frog Squat' as I called it. A grand plié, and I saw how Jarlath watched her. Typical. Her eyes glanced into mine before she spun. She'd explain it away. After all she had to have something to do, otherwise she'd be bored.

I watched another five arabesques before I yawned. Karen perked her arse into a bow. Aoife applauded. Jarlath whistled, stumbled over to her and kissed her face. She shrugged him away as I reached for my drink.

'Whiskey,' said Aoife from her armchair.

'Always.' I drank it quick.

'How's Daddy?' She smiled at me while I breathed through my mouth.

'Fine.'

Karen sat down and hooked her arm through mine. She patted the bunch of letters in my pocket.

'What's this, babe?'

I shoved her hand away. 'Nothing.'

She stood up and bit my cheek, swooped and grabbed the whiskey bottle.

'Guest privileges, Aoife. I'll buy you another.' She pulled me after her but Jarlath got in the way.

'Jarlath,' she said and patted her fingers along his cheek. 'If we weren't such a couple, you'd be such a relief.'

Outside in the hall, things happened quick but in slow motion. I was following Karen but walked into Medb. My hands went to her waist and I felt her face reach my chest. My fingers dug in. Seconds … then she withdrew.

'Did I frighten you?' I said.

She looked at me. 'Not completely,' she said.

Karen pulled me away. We climbed the stairs to our room and once inside I refilled our glasses and drank a full one before complimenting Karen.

'Nice dance. Good configuration.'

'Choreography, arsehole.'

'Mad at me?'

She stood, hand on hips: 'Are you going to spend the whole night drinking?'

I raised the half-empty bottle and Karen sat down on the bed beside me, slopping her drink on her rolled-up skirt.

'Cute legs,' I said.

'Get lost.'

'Even cuter arse,' I whispered into her ear.

She looked at me. 'All for your benefit.'

'What about Jarlath?'

'Pervert-boy?' She shuddered. 'And as for Aoife—there's something too girly about her.'

'Yeah, well. Maybe she has problems.'

'Yeah, well, nothing and I saw you down there.'

'Saw what?'

'No fucking denials, you prick. I saw what you did down there with that Medb one.'

'She unbalanced me.'

'Sure she did.' Karen pointed her toes to stretch her feet, then moved to sit on her side of the bed and picked up postcards from her bedside table. She looked at me. 'Come on.'

' "Having a wonderful time," ' I dictated as she wrote. ' "Everything beyond our wildest dreams. Noah is in his element and I'm bored witless." Three exclamation marks.'

'Finish your drink,' she ordered and signed her name.

'Need to piss,' I said and went into the bathroom.

I avoided the mirror but stood at the sink and gripped its cool ceramic edge.

Things are manageable, I whispered to myself. Devise the schedule and ask the questions. Peel him away. Get behind that goddamned skull.

'Saving's for fools,' I repeated and looked up into the mirror.

Tom stared back. Big, blown-up and just like me. I tried a wink and then I tried a smile. The whiskey had dried my mouth but I spat anyway and I watched the measly spit bubble travel down the glass.

I imagined where Medb's head fit my chest.

Mr Gilmore—you may pay a visit.

Mr Gilmore—you may come.

Preferred it if she had put it like that.

You may come.

I liked the orderly sound of that.

Her face resting on my chest, my fingers digging in her waist and her reply.

Not completely.

I liked the sound of that as well.

IT WAS DARK. Early morning and the kitchen window stared out onto the darker garden. I sat at the table and jotted down my plan.

Grease up old Belios. Compliment and use the valued tool of being a mini devil's advocate. Everyone loves to be questioned—not too much, not when their glamour is on the line—yet they all appreciate the strategic kudos gained by a little shit stirring. Everyone admits to a past, just make sure it's well packaged.

Obstacles: Medb. I could feel her in my gut. I glanced up as if to see her beside me but found myself caught by my reflection in the shiny chrome fridge door. I smiled and watched my mouth stretch. This is what happens. Get old and you see things. You feel shit inside you. All the shit you don't need.

Karen's voice behind me: 'You're hiding.'

The bundle of letters landed on the table in front of me.

'Letters from a fraud,' I said.

Karen sat down, picked up one and hit me on the head with it.

'Not even seven-year-olds say this kind of shit. This … is not you.'

'Might be.'

'Don't try that on me. Won't work. All this crap. How long was it going on for?'

'Six months.'

'Jesus.'

'I'm even seeing a psychiatrist.'

'What?'

'Yeah,' I said. 'None of the—"goddess let's get naked with the local wizard"—but a real doctor in a real office and we talk.'

'About what?'

'About everything.'

'Including these?'

'Told her I had a friend.'

'What does she say?'

'Says I'm normal.'

'Well, there you are then.'

I turned a few of the envelopes so that the addresses faced me.

'Karen, tell me what I was like a year ago.'

'The usual,' she said.

'Still am?'

'Usually … Has she given you tablets?'

'Yeah.'

'Where do you have them?'

'In with my razor.'

Karen placed one hand flat against my cheek while the other traced the long, huge veins on the back of my hands.

'Sorry for hitting you,' she said.

'Usually I enjoy it,' I said.

'Will the tablets keep you sane?'

'Yeah.'

'Stop any nightmares?'

'Every one,' I assured her.

Karen trawled the letters into a messy pile.

'Get rid of them.'

'Fine.'

She pointed at the red words on one envelope. 'The bitch thinks she knows you.'

'Impossible, Karen.'

'Dead fucking right it's impossible. Tear them all up and burn them in the sink.'

I shredded the letters and dumped the remnants into the sink. Karen handed me the lighter and I set fire to my words. I wanted my mind to be blank so I squeezed Karen's hand. I squeezed hard enough to hurt her and she cried out but I kept on squeezing until there was only ash and then I turned on the tap.

Both of us jammed the ash down the plughole.

I sloshed the sink clean then kissed Karen's crushed hand.

She grabbed my hair and pulled my face close to hers.

'As soon as we get back, Noah, you're going to the hairdressers and cooling off the drink.'

I looked at her narrow, dancer's neck and she recognized the look. She smiled and pushed her face close so I could smell her.

'Let's play demons, darling man. Let's play demons and fuck.'

3

NEXT MORNING, I avoided breakfast and got drunk instead. 'No smoking,' the barman had warned me as I reached for a cigarette.

'Fuck off,' I whispered behind my smile.

I like being drunk. I like what it does to me. It warms me, settles into me and makes me real. I said this to Claire. She stuck the crutch label onto it. She called it the Sweetheart Method.

'What?'

She leaned forward and her knees slunk beyond her skirt hem. Hey Claire ... Hey Claire ... Hey Claire ... Hey. She never did do the ladylike thing of pulling her hem forward but allowed her knees to shine out at me. That's how I got the idea of raping her. Like drink, it settled into me and I even thought of confessing. Hey Claire, want to know what I think? I think your knees are telling me something. They keep me interested. Keep me perked.

'The Sweetheart Method?'

Her necklace swung with her perfume. 'My pet name for it,' she explained. 'We all have a Sweetheart Method. We take drugs, drink, have dangerous sex or climb mountains with just our feet and fingernails ... we think we're safe from ordinary life that way. It's never real; it just seems to be. Sooner or later, it suffocates you.'

'Hey Claire, I do bad things.'

'Such as?'

'I beat Karen. She likes it that way so I beat her more. We play games so I can love her enough. We both prefer it that way.'

'You have issues with women?'

'Possibly.'

'Do you like women?'

'Sure.'

'Why?'

I smiled hard at Claire. I really hadn't a fucking clue how to answer and I knew where the whole thing was going ... back to Mammy and love at the breast. Oh Jesus, could I have my fun with my Claire. Hey Claire. Hey Claire. Mammy fucked me up with Daddy's help. I'm a classic case. Feed me the drugs. Teach me the breathing techniques and I'll be normal after all.

At last I said, 'They smell good and they are usually softer.'

'Yes?'

'Yeah. And deep down, I've this thirst for salvation. Find a good one; be saved. Karen doesn't even come close.'

'Does she know this?'

'No.'

Claire's nylon knees buzzed when she crossed them. 'I blame Plato. His story of a soul seeking its cut-away mate—it isn't the truth but we all believe it anyway. We save ourselves. It's got nothing to do with anyone else.'

'Sure,' I said.

I could feel the bang of her thighs against her Chinese cupboard. I could feel me slither in her sweat and fear but I never admitted the rape dreams. Instead I agreed to the three months and ended up in Oughterard, in a pub.

Brilliant drunk that I am, my Sweetheart Method has a method. I drink until I feel the first warmth in my veins, until my surroundings cloud and I stumble to the gents and stare at my greying hair and baggy face.

I should have been something more. Yeah? Well when I'm drunk that something more shines the whole fucking way through. It lights up my eyes. It grabs me and won't let me go. It says, Here I am. It says, This is you.

In the pub, I drank in patient, slow moves while the barman eyed me now and again.

I drank as I jotted down the description of Belios' goblin spine and his face as it had stared at me holding the photograph of his younger self. His grey shedding skin and his eyes staring at his young black and white face.

I closed my eyes to remember his face. I remembered I had imagined his skull seeping through until it eclipsed his features; I remembered his eyes, slit with yellow sleep on his eyelashes; I remembered how I wanted those eyes to turn to me and when they did, I knew I had got to him. You can't fake that. You can't fake seeing yourself as you used to be. Everyone knows that.

I lit a cigarette and an American family a few tables down, eating chips and drinking Coke, scowled over at me. The barman had disappeared for a minute. I inhaled and saluted ash at them. They were the usual fat Yanks, scrubbed clean and affronted. Their little ball-of-dough daughter got to her feet, locked her eyes on me and said, 'Please, Sir. Put that out.'

'Can't. Enjoy it too much.'

She spouted tears and her father yelled at me.

I gazed at the sad little girl and decided to engage her daddy in conversation. I stamped out the cigarette and smiled with my hands wide open.

'Hey,' I called over to him. 'How do you find the Irish?'

His wife covered for his shock, smiled and said: 'You're really just beautiful.'

She meant it. She was pretty and ready to forgive me so I kept smiling and winked at their daughter.

'Enjoying it?'

'Yeah,' said the husband.

'Absolutely,' said the pretty wife.

I nodded at their food. 'We call them chips.'

'We know,' said the husband.

'Ever get round to forgiving the French? Or are they still Free-dom Fries to you?'

The husband rolled to his feet but his wife stopped him. She had soft, round hands to hold him down.

'Stop it, Ed. Stop it. Just be calm. He's a drunken tramp, so for-get him. Finish up,' she ordered her daughter. She tidied up the table, then shooed her daughter towards the pub door and shoved her hus-band to follow.

The door slammed hard behind them and I returned to my drink. Seconds or minutes later—not sure how many but soon enough—Medb stood in front of me.

'You know this drunk?' called the barman.

I raised my hand to see Medb properly and said: 'Fucking hospi-tality here has gone to the dogs.'

'Evan doesn't like drunk people,' Medb said as she wrapped her bag's strap around the chair.

'Evan's a fool,' I told her.

'I'm getting a drink,' she told me and walked over to the bar. Evan had a moon face and red hair. He touched Medb's shoulder and kissed her cheek. I heard him ask after everyone at the house: How's the work? How's life? How's the dad?

I rose to my feet and joined them.

'Introduce me, Medb.'

Evan's fat smile disappeared.

'Evan, this is Mr Gilmore. Mr Gilmore, this is Evan Doyle.'

Medb had a few fifty-euro notes in her hand and she handed over two of them, which Evan put into his pocket. She saw me notice.

'Expensive tastes, Medb?' I said.

'Sit down, Mr Gilmore, and I'll bring you a drink.'

'Evan knows what I like,' I said. I looked around, 'Lovely pub, Evan. Yours?'

'Sit down, Mr Gilmore,' said Medb.

'Call me Noah, then I'll sit.'

Medb had folded the remaining fifty-euro notes into each other and put them into her purse. She looked straight at Evan and said: 'Noah will have the same as before and I'll have orange juice.'

I sat back down.

I watched Medb wait for the drinks. I watched how one of her shoes slid along the foot rail then back again to meet her other shoe. Evan disappeared again, came back with a crate of bottles and I wasn't drunk enough to miss him palm something tiny into her hand. He said something to her and then Medb looked over at me.

Whenever I want to imagine Medb's face, there it is. Not in any other look or moment but there in an early afternoon pub when she turned to look at me, drunk in some corner and sopping up drink with my jacket cuff. If she had smiled, she'd have ruined the moment. She stared at me as Evan poured my drink, took the money she offered and came back with change. I liked the stare. It meant I was in her sights.

Medb sat down opposite me and I felt her legs steer sideways from mine. She put her purse back into her bag and sipped her orange juice before looking at me.

'Evan's the boyfriend?' I said.

'A friend.'

'He doesn't like me.'

'Well, you're drunk.'

'So he says.'

'Evan and Jarlath went to school together. He likes to keep in touch.'

'So he gave you something for Jarlath.' I nodded at her hand. 'He likes you.'

Medb sipped her drink again. 'Evan likes everybody.'

'Not like you, huh? You can't stand me ... which seems a bit weird since according to your father, you're the one who invited me.'

'He didn't mean it literally, Mr Gilmore.'

'Noah. Remember?' I gulped too quickly at my whiskey and pig-snorted it back onto the table. 'Jesus, sorry. Did I get you? Fuck ... No, I'll clean it up ...' I used my jacket cuff again, all the time talking, all the time forcing her attention onto me and not the wet table. 'Literally? What kind of excuse is that? You wrote the invitation and what do you know ... I came.' I shook my sodden jacket arm into the air. 'Makes me feel I was got here on false pretences.'

'You're not really necessary … Noah.'

'I'm going to make your father famous again.'

'You think that's what he wants?'

'Doesn't everybody? Look Medb, think of the "dribble-effect".'

'Which is?'

'You're bright, Medb. You know.'

'I don't need my father's fame.'

I lifted my glass and sloshed the whiskey before swallowing some down. I looked at her calm, pale face and said: 'If I'm drunk and let's say I am, I could also be paranoid and suspect you've being following me.'

'And if I have?'

'I think you're afraid.'

'I'm not afraid.'

'Well, it's to be expected. You're the oldest, right? Maybe there's stuff you don't want to come out in the wash? Maybe you're afraid I'll fuck up and make you look fools. Or maybe I won't. Maybe I'll be fucking brilliant and open you up to the world.'

'I've read your work,' Medb said.

'So?'

'So, you haven't got what I need.'

In my drunk, devil-may-care slur of a mind, her words zeroed in and shrivelled my grin. I leaned back against the wall, all the better to see her. I tried to smile any shit kind of smile as long as I could frighten her but somehow I was fucked.

'My, what a harsh bitch you are.'

'I said to my father—if this is all that can find you, then put him out of his misery. Tell him your story.'

'And I'm supposed to be grateful, right?'

'You're supposed to do your job.'

'Join the dots?'

'If you can.'

'Your father wants me here,' I said. I paused to get my words right—stuck them up inside my mind where I could see them before I said them. 'He wants a professional biography of his life. Fuck the dots. I can write down every word to describe how he's lived his life.

I'll use everything he has done; put it down in black and white and make it perfect.'

'That's not possible,' said Medb.

'Fuck you,' I replied.

I drank the last of my whiskey and remembered what she had said: 'How come I'm not what you need?'

Medb untwisted her bag from the chair and put its strap across her shoulders. I reached forward and caught the strap in my fist. 'That's a shit thing to say.'

She glanced down at my hand then up at my face:

'Your Karen. Is she supposed to love you?'

'What else?' I said.

I wound the strap tighter and I saw Medb wince as part of it bit into her shoulder but she answered me back.

'Jarlath will be disappointed.'

'Jarlath can fuck himself,' I said.

I had caught the strap between my thumb and forefinger, then wound it round my fist. My skin had gone red. It would have gone red at her shoulders. I looked at her face and I longed to kiss her. I must have reached my face up because her eyes changed, softened into wariness, the sort of wariness that turns me on.

'Last night,' I reminded her. 'I asked you if I frightened you and you replied: "Not completely." That's not the sort of answer you give to a man you don't need anything from.'

I drove all the sex I could muster into my smile and yelled out Evan's name. Evan swung his fat face in my direction and he saw what I was doing. Before he could move I said: 'Another whiskey, Evan.'

'You okay, Medb?' said Evan.

I let Medb go and she nodded for Evan's benefit. She pulled her blouse straight at her shoulder, then looked at me.

'What has he promised you?' she said.

'Writer/subject confidentiality.'

'That sounds good,' she said.

'I think so too,' I agreed.

'No matter what he promises, it'll mean nothing in the end.'

'It'll mean his story is out there. That's all he needs.'

Medb picked up her glass, put it down again. She stood up. Evan brushed past her and I suppose they touched because he had eyes only for her face and she half-smiled at him. He put my drink on the table.

'Hey Medb,' I said. Hey Medb. Hey Medb, I thought.

'What?'

Evan wanted to wait, just fucking itching to hear what I'd say to her, how she'd react, maybe she'd even fucking smile at me and ruin his wet dreams but I said nothing until he got the hint and went back to his bar.

'How did you feel growing up and never seeing a photograph of yourself?'

Medb looked straight at me and shrugged.

'It's the way things were.'

'Not exactly normal,' I said.

'Not exactly,' she said and walked away.

I watched her back as she reached the pub's door and I knew there was no fucking way she'd look back at me but I didn't take my eyes off her, not until she absolutely disappeared.

Round one to both of us, I decided.

Within half an hour I had found another pub and was on the mobile to Claire.

'Thought you might like to know—I'm feeling good and my friend is feeling good.'

'Noah …'

'Oh shit … you've a client. Why didn't I think of that? Well, this friend's got a great story for me and he's got three kids. Their mother's dead and they're all a little bit fucked up but who doesn't want to be these days?'

'Ten seconds, Noah.'

'One of the kids looks right into me. Ever had that, Claire? Maybe she's heard of Plato too? Makes fucking sense when I think about it. What are you telling the victim in your room? How fucking incredible life can be if you just do it anyway? Hey Claire … Hey Claire … Know what I do? Know how I get through the nights? Shit … Fine … cut me off.'

In the toilets I tried to vomit. I hacked up lager-and-whiskey flavoured phlegm and nothing else. I splashed water into my eyes and when I glanced up at my reflection, I could hardly see.

Madness I know. Fucked up and brilliant and making me live inside. I was drunk with it and found myself outside Oughterard and on the bog road where I was completely the lone live thing. I retched up colourless bile into the ditch, lost my balance, skidded and spun back into standing position.

Silence. A low grass-level wind and the sun blasted red in the late afternoon. I laughed out loud at the poetics of it all. Fuck me, I needed a camera. The sky was undressing itself. And I thought of the one fantastic thing I could do. I'd do what Belios had never done— photograph what he had ignored and make an art out of it.

So I bought a camera and returned to show it to Karen. I swung it into the room before me and it landed on the bed.

Karen looked up from a self-help book.

'About bloody time.'

I bowed. 'Your cock has returned.' I nodded at the book. 'Not like you to read.'

'It's supposed to be good.' Karen said. 'Everyone's reading it. It's supposed to change your life.'

I took off my jacket. 'What the fuck for?'

'For the better.' Karen turned a page and drew her legs into the armchair. 'You look like shit. Wash before you even think of coming near me.'

I threw myself at her feet, took one foot in my hand and licked an uneven line from her big toe to her ankle. She kept her eyes on the page but I knew where to get her: a spot of very soft flesh in her high instep. I licked and bit and she screeched. She pushed her feet into my face and her eyes flashed happy. She dropped the book and purred as I kissed along her legs until she hit me.

From that point on it was the usual. I wouldn't let her scream and she wouldn't let me grunt. We grappled and sweated on the carpet. I made her hips judder and jammed my fists at her head and neck. She bit and tried to kiss me. I watched her mouth under mine, dark red and waiting. I kissed, forced her mouth wide and her neck strained and I heard her low, long squeal …

'Hallelujah,' she said afterwards.

'Great,' I said. I searched my clothes for cigarettes. 'Any fags?'

Karen didn't open her eyes but she shook her head.

'I liked it.'

I stepped over her to reach the bed and shoved my hand under the pillows.

'Found some. Liked what?'

I lit two and went to hand her one but she moved onto to her side and began doing leg-lifts.

'Those few minutes, darling man.'

'Jesus, thanks.'

'Don't be mad.'

'I'm not mad. Do I sound mad?'

'Now you sound like a prick.'

I twirled the camera. 'Your grey-haired prick and his new toy. What do you think?'

'Don't make me lose count. Seventeen one thousand … eighteen one thousand … nineteen one thousand … twenty. That's a camera? Looks like a mini-camera. Does its thing move in and out?'

'Very fucking funny. It's a telescopic lens.'

'Could you not have got something cheaper? You're not a photographer.' She turned on her stomach and did some yoga move. 'Is that part of the plan? Sweet-talk the old bastard and show him what a fan you are?'

'Exactly. Stop doing that shit, will you?'

Karen got up. 'It's not shit. It's my life.' She pulled on a slip and clipped her hair up. 'Where did you disappear to?'

'The village.'

'And its pubs?'

'Couldn't just leave them standing there.'

'Taking me out to dinner?'

'Definitely.'

'Good. I'm going to have a shower. Hey … you?'

I looked over and winked. She came close, winked back and kissed me.

As she straightened up she said: 'Oh, strange thing. That Medb one drew me today. Didn't want a ballet pose … just me doing fucking nothing but sitting under a tree. Seemingly she's a shit-hot illustrator ready for the big time. Aoife says she gets it from her dad.'

I didn't fucking move.

'She drew you?'

'Yeah, she drew me. Don't look at me like that, Noah. Anyone would think you're interested. Shit … is that my phone?'

'I'm the fucking biographer, Karen. Of course I'm interested.'

'Oh yeah … God forbid you'd be thinking of fucking her.' Karen flipped open her phone. 'Look, Anita, I can't talk just now. I'll ring you later. Yeah, bye.' She looked at me. 'I'm having a shower. Want to share?'

'Fine.'

We showered in silence and I didn't even think and every time Medb came into my head, I shut her down. I willed her into nothing. I smiled into Karen's eyes and made sure she smiled back. Easy. Easy. The whole damn thing should be easy.

We both got drunk. I drank to keep my stomach busy while Karen just wanted to do something normal. She drank in large gulps.

'This reminds me of home,' she said. 'Can't drink in that haunted house.'

'You managed last night,' I told her.

'Why aren't you eating?' she said.

'Don't know.'

She leaned in, see-sawing her plate with one elbow. 'Jesus!' She brushed potato off her arm. 'How much more time in this tourist shit-hole? I swear to Christ, Noah—it's doing my head in.'

'You're not fucking stranded here, Karen. Go home if you want.'

'If I were a bitch, I'd leave you.'

'So I'm safe.'

Karen shrugged. 'So you are.'

'Karen …'

'What?'

'Tell me about the drawing?'

Karen helped herself to mint sauce. 'What drawing?'

I smiled into her fake innocent stare. 'The one where you sat under a tree.'

'Ah, that one? Shit ... that was nothing to write home about.'

'You said ...'

'Yeah, I know what I said ... but as far as I'm concerned art survives on individual appreciation and hers didn't qualify. I thought it was crap.'

'Why?'

'Why the dog with a bone, Noah?'

'I'm just interested, Karen.'

'Oh yeah, right. Last night was interesting too. I saw how you looked at her and I heard what she said. Don't think I don't notice these things.'

'I just wanted to know if you thought she was any good,' I said.

'I want more wine,' said Karen. She looked for the waiter, ordered another bottle then switched back to me.

'You forget things, Noah ... You know that? You forget I can see you and now and again I see the odd thing.'

Medb's face in my chest. My hands on her waist.

'Like now,' said Karen.

I refilled my glass. 'Like now?'

'Just now you were thinking of her.'

'I just wondered about the fucking drawing. Jesus—I'll take your word for it ... it was crap. I suppose you got rid of it?'

'Yeah, I did.'

'Why did she draw you, Karen?'

'Haven't the foggiest. You'd left me alone. Thanks a lot for that, by the way. Aoife was ignoring me, Jarlath was leering and Medb just turned up. Took one look at me and said she'd like to draw me. And who was I to say no? After all she's the daughter of some famous guy and I'm just a hanger-on.'

'I saw her today,' I said.

'I'll bet you did.'

'She called you my Karen.'

'Did she?'

Karen hiccuped and took another drink.

'Where the fuck is dessert?'

After dinner, we made our way to the riverbank and smoked hash in silence until Karen said, 'Jesus fucking Christ,' into the darkness.

'Where?'

Karen shook her head. She was lying on her back, one arm raised and swaying with the joint in her hand. Red ash flakes spun and I watched the bend of her elbow, the semi-arch of her arm; how her palm cupped into a flower shape and I inched forward and sat cross-legged with my face above hers.

'Where's the bastard?' I said.

She shook her head again and my guts froze because her eyes shone up into mine. Fuck you, I thought and fuck those eyes. Her fingers reached up and pinched along my face.

'Why do you love me so much when I'm drunk, Noah?'

'I just do.'

Karen shifted so her breasts rose. 'You like all of me when I'm drunk.'

'Every bit,' I said.

'Don't lie.' Karen's fingers were hurting me so I hurt back. She began to cry so I kissed her and she dragged at my shoulders to pull me down. I stretched out alongside her and stroked her face.

'What was it like, Karen?'

Karen closed her eyes and I was very careful. I stroked her cheeks and forehead, murmured nonsense close to her ears. Hey ... Hey ... Hey ... I practised in my head until I thought I had it right.

'Hey ... Hey ...' I said. 'It's only a drawing. I bet she used felt-tip pens.'

I placed my hand between Karen's nearly there breasts and she liked that. She touched my hand and she tried to push her fingers beneath mine. I curled my hand around hers and kissed her fingers. She opened her eyes.

'It was exactly me, Noah.'

'And you destroyed it.'

'Hey ... Hey ... Hey ...' she said.

'What?'

'How come you don't love me anymore?'

Something slid inside me. Call it a demon ... a slithering, mad little bastard that smells hunger. Never really mentioned that to Claire. I like hunger and it's got everything to do with the eyes. I like hunger when it's right in front of me, desperate and wanting whatever I can give it. It's like prising the guts from a live fish, feeling its heart still beat and watching its crazy eye swivel to meet mine. In moments like these I imagine I could be a saviour.

THE TRUTH IS drunks prefer each other. It's a slimy pact but it does its job.

I put Karen to bed then searched the room for the drawing. I even looked among my notes. I thought maybe even Karen would have a sense of dramatic humour. Nothing. Nothing in the wastepaper basket; nothing under her pillow or in her suitcase, then I went into the bathroom and found it burnt to a crisp in the sink.

I cupped my hands about it and tried to coax it onto the counter. Wisps of ash floated from it but finally it lay beside the sink. I stared at the curled-up, ash-black flimsy paper for a long time. I moved my head around every angle but there was nothing left to see.

Medb looked at me in the pub. It meant I was in her sights.

Your Karen? Is she supposed to love you?

I slapped my hand down and crushed what was left. I tore off some toilet paper and cleaned it up, turned the cold tap on full blast and dunked my head in. The water rushed onto the back of my neck and I stayed there until I couldn't stand it anymore. Towel-dried my hair and I went back to Karen.

She was burping in her sleep. I sat beside her with my new camera in my hands.

I held the camera to my eye and felt its heft in my hands. Karen stirred in her sleep and her knee dug into my back. I turned and looked at her.

Belios never photographed sleeping people. He wanted their eyes open, staring into him as if they could physically peel them away. The old bastard knew what he was doing. Fuck the art—right, William? Grab that face. Jam it against the light, against any kind of fucking shadow. Find that blasted humanity that tells you the whole mirage is worth it.

Karen burped again. I flicked my lighter and angled my body closer, all the more to feel her heat because I was shaking and the light shivered and my thumb was burning, but I didn't stop there. Fuck no. Inside me was that sick, unnerving glee and fighting it in the back of my head was my voice saying something normal: saying, Come on, you prick. Stop it now. End the fucking games. Kiss the drunken girlfriend and get the fuck out.

How come don't you love me anymore?

I love you for all the reasons you thought you could stomach. I love you because you drink with me. I love you because we're somehow safe.

I looked through the lens at Karen's face. The camera followed the lighter's flame over her nose, her lips, her forehead and then her eyes. Did Medb see all this? The lighter lit up the pathway towards the bedroom door and for one moment I thought, I can't be bothered. Get downstairs and find the whiskey. I ignored the thought. I nudged Karen's head until it lay straight on her pillow, until her whole body lay straight and then I lifted my body onto hers.

This close, I sweated more. My hips slid a little and the camera angle slipped back. My hands were shaking so much that I bit into them to force them still. The pain made me focus on Karen's face. Karen had always been beautiful. Milk-white child's face, the same as when I had met her. Too fucking young, I had thought, until she had me to herself and I heard her voice and watched her eyes. She did something beautiful too. She stood close beside me on her tiptoes and placed her head under my chin. I smelled her perfume and dance-club sweat and she said: 'Let's pretend anything you want.'

I sat up on her hips and clicked, keeping a check on how much I used, but my hands soon trembled beyond my control and I dropped the camera right onto Karen's chest. She jackknifed upwards and I shoved the camera out of sight as her face slammed into mine.

She yelled as her head bounced back. I rolled onto my side of the bed and she landed on her pillow.

'Oh Christ, my nose. I think I'm bleeding, Noah!'

'You're not bleeding.'

'Turn on the light, Noah, and look at me!'

I did. 'It's just a little red. There's no blood. You'll survive.'

Karen moved her head from side to side and tapped her fingers along the bridge of her nose.

'It could have a hairline crack. If it does, it could change my profile.'

I shrugged and reached over for a cigarette from the bedside table.

'I think you should stop smoking,' Karen said as I lit up. She sat, pressed against the headboard. 'It's bad for you, makes you sick looking. And I think we should both stop drinking. I think when we get back home, we'll have to implement changes.'

'I don't know if I'm interested enough, Karen.'

Karen said nothing to that. I heard her breath fizz in and out and when I glanced up, she was staring out into the body of the dark room. I got off the bed, left the room to smoke in peace on the landing.

I imagined Claire and the fantasy juiced through me but then I pictured the long, covered body of Medb, the colour of her face, her breasts and her waist.

Fuck me, I craved.

A door opened somewhere down the hall but I ignored it. A mirror hung above a small table and I blew smoke onto my reflection. It was the sort of face not many people wanted to see anymore. Even Jerry, my publisher, had been afraid the last time. He mentioned plastic surgery as well as the gym and a nutritious diet. Necessary restoration, he told me. Decadence had a shelf life and I was too fucking old to hack the pace anymore. He dressed it up and told me he was worried. I told him I had other plans. I grinned with my big mouth in my big head and I told him I quit. I told him I had other plans. I was so fucking out of it on bravado that I told him my dream. Write the biography of the photographer who disappeared into the wild west of Ireland. Write in big beautiful words and in such a way that people can only be amazed. Write it down so that I can see him. Open up Belios. See what's inside. See what made him.

My shaking hands made my whole body shake in front of Jerry and my spit was flying. Jerry was transfixed and I almost more so because of this wild delight inside of me, this shit-stirring happiness that meant I was alive. I was scary with it. Words jammed my mouth and wouldn't come out. I worked my mouth like a fish and nothing came. Jerry remained seated, pressed a button and rang for his secretary.

He began talking to me and said I was tired. Maybe I just needed a rest. The last book had done me proud. Take a sip of water now—that's good. All you need is a rest. Be right as rain again. No, don't apologize. We all get these moments, eh? Christina, get him more water. Jesus—is he okay? Oh fucking Christ—do we have to get a doctor?

But I calmed down. I drank as much water as Christina offered me and I listened to Jerry as he told me about this psychiatrist, Claire Shepard. Absolutely brilliant. Did wonders for the wife.

I once told Claire that people didn't really hide their faces and she had acted surprised. A psychological trick of hers but I liked her tricks; they made me want to talk.

'We all wear masks,' she said. 'We can thank the Greeks for that.'

But I wanted to explain to her, look right into her professional mask and say, Jesus, Claire—hasn't life fucked you up enough to know that masks are the excuse—that all you need is the guts to keep your face real?

Course she'd never fucking buy it. It would ruin her business.

My big bad face with its overblown skin stared back at me.

'You could look handsome if you really tried,' Karen said from the doorway.

Another noise and a door closed. I heard Karen move behind me and say, 'Hi, Jarlath.'

I turned and saw him three feet from Karen, carrying a hot-water bottle.

'How's your dad?' Karen said.

'Waiting for Noah,' Jarlath replied.

Karen winked at me. 'There, you see? Use that as your book title: "Waiting For Noah."' She walked over to the banister, leaned over on her stomach.

'Anyone ever fall over, Jarlath?' Karen asked.

'No.'

She craned her neck up at the ceiling. 'Love these old houses. Feels as if you spend your whole life being minded by them. You must love that.'

'Jarlath's going travelling, Karen. Can't be that in love with the place.'

'It was my mother's house,' said Jarlath. 'When she died, we came back.' He walked past us and down the stairs towards the kitchen. Karen came up close to me and hooked her fingers into my belt. I hated those fucking moments when she believed gentleness would get me in the end.

THE PEOPLE I am used to dealing with ... well, they're used to dealing with me. It's like a bargain, a deal of understanding: you display me in the best light possible, magic my vices into something worth loving and never forget I'm the star. I'm the one people are supposed to envy, love, lust after and forgive—and the biographer me—well, I get taken in. I get told stories. I get to believe them for a while. I get to play with words. I get to imagine I'm in the heads of these people and that they actually mean something to me. As I said, it's a bargain.

A celebrity-biographer has one subject and the rest, as Belios would say, are additions. The additions have their place. Mother, father, brother, sister, lover, child, secret skeleton in the closet—all need to be used in the right place, the right moment and what they have to say has to dovetail with the subject's memory but never at the expense of personality.

Unless the subject is well dead and people are actually interested in the why and how he/she lived their lives. With that kind of life, there's always a more brilliant story. The information of such lives has history, time and experience to whet the story: make it gold; make it live.

The kind of information I dealt with was a few steps above the trash titbits in glossy gossip magazines, usually more concerned with cellulite and sweat-stains of favourite celebrities—their Botoxed masks, orange skin and insatiable need to be adored. A few steps above such shit and its questions of a quasi-spiritual nature. How God figures into everything. How drugs and drink can ruin your soul. How the man/woman/whatever that I fucked last night is actually my soul mate and you see, Plato was right after all and for that reason *Hello* magazine are photographing our wedding.

Above that level it's something different. The additions are still there but they have to be handled with extra care and the information sometimes needs to be whittled out, carved out of words that on their own might promise nothing but it's how they're put down that spark me and spark the story.

Jarlath had made tea and was sitting at the kitchen table. He said nothing while I made coffee. I sat down opposite him, poured milk into my coffee and he gestured to where the sugar bowl sat next to the jam and butter on the table.

'Thanks,' I said.

I stirred the sugar in, blew across my mug and took a gulp. 'The "Waiting for Noah" bit—that was just a joke,' I apologized. 'Karen gets a bit bored now and again. She's a ballerina, you know, not too interested in my side of things. It was a bit of a row you walked into there.'

Jarlath shrugged and kept on drinking his tea.

'So how do you think I should play this, Jarlath?'

'What?'

'Your father's biography. How should I dive in?'

'That's up to you, isn't it?'

'I kind of feel I'm up against it though.'

'Really?'

'Yeah.' I put down my mug, leaned forward just a little and said, 'I kind of get the feeling that I'm not welcome.' I shrugged. 'It's natural. Who likes their lives pried open? Causes hassle for most, extreme embarrassment for a few. It's just that at the end of it all, it could be to everyone's advantage.'

'Like money?' said Jarlath.

'Like money. Like fame. Like the ability to finally travel the world, which is what you want to do, isn't it? That's what Aoife told me.'

'Yeah.'

'Continue your father's legacy?' I prompted. 'Be an explorer and experience the kinds of things people are too afraid to? Ever read Willard Price, Jarlath?'

'Who's he?'

'A writer. I was mad about his stories when I was a kid.'

'Two boys,' I said. 'Hal and Roger. Daddy was some anthropologist or something and he had this idea that in order for his sons to experience real life, he had to take them out of school for a whole year and make them see what went on in the real world—which consisted of Africa, the South Seas—I can't remember if they did America—I was really only interested in Africa, because of your father. But this guy Willard Price, he whetted my appetite too. Tsavo National Park, the Serengeti, Rift Valley, the Masai, Madagascar, Malindi, Mombasa, Dar Es Salaam, Mount Kilimanjaro. Am I making you homesick, Jarlath?'

'I don't remember much.'

'Know what I learned from Willard Price?'

'What?'

I leaned in, smiled. 'How to navigate whales.'

Jarlath coughed down his tea. 'Yeah, sure.'

'No, serious. You have to imagine it. You've got a good imagination, haven't you, Jarlath?'

'Yeah. Yeah. Great.'

'Whaling ship ... let's say off Japan ... I mean those bastards have no idea about protecting a precious species ... Hal and Roger on this ship ... these huge chunks of whale-back blubber have been dug out in a row and Hal is stepping into each hole. Like walking the whale's backbone. There's blood and blubber-fat swimming on the deck and the crew are yelling and laughing. Sweat and sea spray and this feel of a huge mammal beneath your feet. Your runners getting soaked with its blood and the hot stink of it all and maybe you're frightened, I mean who the fuck wouldn't be?

'Then something happens and you're cut adrift from the ship. Your younger brother is back on the ship and you're stranded on the back of hacked-into whale, in the middle of the ocean and presumably you're going to die ... so what's the solution?'

'Haven't a clue,' said Jarlath.

'Well,' I said. 'If you had been Hal, he being his father's son and possessing his father's initiative, you would have navigated the whale right back to the ship.'

'Yeah, right,' said Jarlath.

'No, serious. You would have dug your fingers into the wounded whale and dragged yourself to the whale's blow-hole, made sure you had a good grip with your legs and then leaned down and blew out on either side of the blow-hole, depending on which way you wanted the whale to turn and there you go: How to Navigate a Whale in ... let's say ... Four Easy Steps.'

'Is that true?'

'I never experienced it but after I read Willard Price's *Whale Adventure*, I wanted to do it.'

'Ever check up on it?' asked Jarlath.

'Why the hell would I want to ruin a good memory like that?'

'It's a good story,' said Jarlath.

'A geography teacher?' I wondered aloud. 'How come you settled for that?'

Jarlath glanced into his mug. 'Just did.'

'Just seemed easier?' I asked.

Jarlath looked up and shrugged. 'We came back here, lived here, went to school here ...'

'Oh, yeah, met a friend of yours today. Evan ... Doyle. A barman. I kind of pissed him off ... smoked for a few seconds. Living in Dublin, you hear all these stories of the smokers' Shangri-La in country pubs ... sorry, go on ... went to school here ...'

'And that's just it. You settle into things.'

I handed Jarlath my cigarette pack.

He took one. His fingertips were dark yellow and the nails were dirty. His face was yellow-green and there was a cold sore on his upper lip. He leaned into my lighter and he smelled of BO.

'Must have pissed you off,' I said. 'Just to settle into things. So geography was the closet thing you could get to exploring?'

'We needed money,' said Jarlath. 'So I finally got a job teaching in the girls' school here.'

'Were you their favourite?'

'What?'

'The girls' favourite teacher—considering who your dad is. A world-famous photographer and explorer. You must have had some mystique about you. All little girls like that.'

'I told them a few things—nothing like your whale story though.'

'Ah well, that's probably not real,' I said. 'Your stories would have been, wouldn't they? All those names I mentioned before—you must remember being there as a little kid, following in your daddy's footsteps—must have been heaven on fucking earth when you look back on it all.'

'We didn't travel with my father.'

'Oh, right. So what did you do then?'

'Stayed at home.'

'Which was where?'

'The Old Town, Mombasa.'

'Mombasa. Yeah … when I was talking to your dad earlier … I saw a photograph of his. "The Fort Jesus." Brilliant image. Shadows of people on the wall and thinking back on it, I wonder was that deliberate?'

'What do you mean?'

'Well, part of your dad's brilliance is that he makes you think. Shadows on the wall … if you look just at them … not the real people but just the shadows … you have to think of the slaves that were kept in the cells hundreds of years ago.'

'It's just a photograph,' said Jarlath.

'But look what it made me think,' I said.

Jarlath rolled his empty mug between his hands.

'And look at what you became,' I said, 'just a geography teacher.'

At the crux of any conversation with an 'addition', two things can happen. The addition can fuck me out of it, spout some privacy shit and leave, or they can swallow, get silent for a few seconds and stay. And why would they do the second thing? Simple—they want something and they've been given a clue how to get it.

'Wasn't my real choice,' said Jarlath.

'I know,' I said. 'You had to help the family. Ditch your dreams for the sake of theirs and make money to pay the bills. Bet your room is full of books on exploration. Hard to imagine there are still areas left to explore.'

'There's always places where people are afraid to go even though somebody has been there before,' said Jarlath.

'Like where?'

'Africa.'

'You'd go back there? Why? It's been done and dusted. The white man's done his business there.'

'I don't mean it like that.'

'No?'

'I'd visit places and I'd visit my mother.'

'Evelyn,' I said.

Jarlath was still rolling the mug between his hands.

'Why did you leave?'

'He wanted to leave.'

Bingo. Fucking lit up neon lights in my head. He wanted to leave. He. Not dad, daddy, father or even papa. He.

'Did he?' I said. 'Probably heartbroken. Didn't want to be reminded of her. Didn't want to live in the same house and expect her to walk through the door at any moment. Good job he had her family home to come back to. Still … it must have been a culture shock.'

Jarlath put his mug down and played his little finger in and out of the mug's handle.

'The weather for one thing,' I continued. 'And the accents, not to mention the whole place was white. You must have been so exotic to the likes of Evan Doyle.'

'I suppose we were,' said Jarlath. He gave a quick smile and I pounced just a little.

'You look like your dad when you do that,' I said.

Jarlath stopped smiling.

'We're used to having people like you find us,' he said.

'What does that mean?'

'Ask Dad … So when does the money find us instead?'

I offered Jarlath another cigarette. He inhaled hard a few times then used his mug as the ashtray.

'Medb drew Karen today,' I said.

Jarlath flicked me a look.

'Karen says she's shit-hot.'

'She is,' said Jarlath.

'Got your dad's artistic genes?'

Jarlath exhaled and nodded.

'What did you get from him besides the yen to explore?'

Jarlath shrugged.

'What about Evelyn?' I asked. 'You must have loved her.'

Jarlath said nothing but shoved his fingers into his mug and screwed down his cigarette butt.

I plastered an understanding smile on my face and I said, 'Someone is taken from you and all you're left with is unfinished business. Did they ever find the murderer?'

'No,' said Jarlath. 'They never found him.'

I filed 'him' with 'he'; all information and all to be used.

I glanced at my coffee and my stomach revolted a little. Patches of milk-grease grime slid on the surface but I swallowed it down. Jarlath was getting to his feet and I stalled him.

'Hey,' I said, as freewheeling as I could manage. 'Your Medb doesn't like me.'

Jarlath turned back from the door. 'That's because she says you haven't the balls.'

That got me. It shut me up. Jarlath left the kitchen and I flung my mug into the sink. Medb and the doll-bitch waist. Medb draws my girlfriend under a tree. You're not what I need. Not completely. Not exactly. Don't have the balls.

Balls for what?

4

KAREN HAD LEFT my medication on the bathroom counter and a note beside it: 'Forgive me and eat these up.'

I screwed up the note and swallowed the pills one by one. Balls for what? kept looping singsong in my head. Balls for what? I turned from the mirror, tripped, slammed forwards and my head cracked on the tiles. Pain shot through me and fixed me down. I blacked out and when I came to, the ceiling zigzagged with light and I vomited up yellow curd and my pills. I turned my face against the floor so I wouldn't suffocate in my own sick. I tried to yell for Karen, but each time there was fresh vomit and then just dry retching until it just hurt to breathe.

I waited until I got used to the smell of sick and then I dragged my body onto all fours and inched upwards with the sink for leverage. I turned on the taps, washed my mouth and face and then I noticed blood diluting in the water. Without raising my head, I pressed about my sticky, wet skull until I felt the cut along the near middle of my head. My gut heaved and I jerked forward. My hands shot out onto the taps to steady myself. I raised my face to check the damage. Crumbs of vomit stuck to the mirror and blood dripped down my face. I grabbed the toilet paper and wiped the blood away to leave a pink sheen.

I wiped the vomit off the mirror, then swallowed the exact amount of pills again, went back into the bedroom and picked up my dictaphone from the desk. I stood there and stared across at sleeping Karen and wondered what else I needed. I remembered drink so I returned to the bathroom, grabbed one of the short glasses left there for teeth-cleaning and went back into the bedroom—found the whiskey, sat on the chair and kept drinking until I felt the same way I always felt when I knew I could do anything.

The room floated with just the right colours and my legs felt warm and good. I felt good. I left the room and walked down the hall towards Belios' room. The hall followed me, its other doors sidled up at my elbows, but when I edged my gaze backwards, there was nothing behind me but the blank carpet and blank silence. I opened Belios' door.

William Belios sat close to a small fire in the grate. The room smelled of his sweat and his dinner. I held up my dictaphone. He nodded and pointed out the chair opposite him. I sat and hissed out a smile despite the pain in my skull.

'Bring cigarettes?' he asked.

I tossed him the packet. 'Your son went through them.'

Belios' fingers shook as put one in his mouth. He dug around his blanket and found a packet of matches and waved away my offer of help.

'Must be hard for your kids to see you like this.'

The old man smiled. He turned his gaze from me to the fire and said: 'Mr Gilmore ...'

'Just use my first name—Noah.'

'Noah ... I'm dying at a fast rate. My children are doing what is considered morally decent. They are waiting. One morning Aoife will find me dead. Jarlath will draw up the funeral bill and Medb will consider it justice done.'

The sound of Medb's name made me want her in the conversation.

'Medb said I hadn't the balls.'

Belios shone his gaze at me, blue veins at his temples and a congealed cluster of sores on his upper lip.

He dangled his cigarette over the edge of his wheelchair arm. 'Medb never gives up on her ideas.'

'You're not smoking your cigarette, William.'

Belios lifted his arm in extra slow motion and his loose pyjama sleeve wrinkled up to his elbow to reveal a withered arm.

'Some sight, isn't it?' said Belios. He sucked at his cigarette. 'The uselessness of old age is always amazing. All these do-gooders who talk about the wonders of advancing years just hoping to Christ they're dead before they get there.'

'What did Medb mean?' I said.

Belios glanced across at me, then down at my crotch. 'Exactly what she said.'

'You've read my letters, William.'

'So I did.'

'And I was invited.'

'Naturally you were.'

'So what's the problem?'

Belios' laugh guttered out in spits of saliva and he moved his fag-holding hand to wipe his mouth.

'Christ,' I said and moved to stop him. I plucked the fag away and into the fire. Belios caught my hand. My knees bumped against his wheelchair and as I tried to stand up he refused to let me go. Instead his other hand rose close to my face then hovered.

He acted like an artist with his newest model, half-reaching as if to touch a feral thing and then deciding to leave it virgin. Like an animal sniffing out its prospects, I bowed my face within inches of Belios' fingers. His teeth sucked in air and his hands trembled. His breath was warm and I half-saw, half-imagined where his fingers skimmed the air above my skin. After seconds he murmured: 'It doesn't fit.'

My skull burned as I withdrew. I licked sweat from my lips and stood as straight as I could manage it. I smiled at Belios and slurred back his own words: 'It doesn't fit?'

Belios shrugged and splayed out his hands. 'Those letters ... that face. That mass of a face. You came with plans to get a camera between my fingers. Get me to see you.' He lifted his hand towards his wall of photographs.

I remained calm and I remained standing. Things were just fine. Things were brilliant.

'Tell me, Noah—how can you have such a face?'

'I grew it this way.'

Each year, I wanted to tell him … each year something turned my face old and I tried to catch up with it but I couldn't. All the people I kissed arse with added wrinkles and punched bags under my eyes; all those blasted, brilliant faces I saw when no one was looking; all those faces I watched and failed to catch just because I couldn't photograph them anymore, they added things as well—whiter hair, the whiskey I can't live without and the drugs.

Belios was still smiling. 'When I received your letters,' he said. 'I thought—here's another one after all these years. Dying men need their succour, Noah, and it's been a long time since I had a visitor.'

I sat back down.

'So you'll survive for the time I'm here?' I said. My skull pounded but I smiled and shifted my gaze about the room.

'Jarlath reminded me that this used to be Evelyn's house.' My gaze jumped with the pain but I hung onto my professional biographer's mask for all it was worth. Belios wasn't some glossy media whore who'd respond to some inane praise. Fuck that. The man was used to parasites.

Belios laid his head back against his headrest and stared at me.

'Tell me, Noah. How would you like me to see you … a clever man who writes letters admiring my work or a fool who writes "I want to be you"?'

Fuck you, Belios. Fuck your family and your dead wife in Africa. I smiled through my teeth while my head pulsated. Don't lose, don't lose, don't lose. I eased up in my chair and held up the dictaphone. 'What do you know? Forgot to turn it on.' I dragged a side-table into the middle between my chair and his, aimed the damn thing, then switched it on.

Belios stared at it and for the first few long seconds all it taped was the fire and my own breathing.

'What do you know of me, Noah?' said Belios.

I reeled it out. 'Born in Ireland. You have never given any real interviews. A wife. Three kids. Lived in Kenya mostly and used it as a base. A priest for some years, then an explorer and photographer. Private man; hailed as some kind of saviour of photography. Portraits. You tried landscapes once or twice and most critics said they lacked power ...'

'Have you ever held a camera, Noah?'

Cut in mid-stream, I swallowed air then said yes.

'With a face like that ... don't you frighten them away?'

I thought of Karen's body under me. 'They never run.'

'How do you keep them?' asked Belios.

'With sweets and promises,' I replied.

Belios gestured towards his gallery. 'Want to know how I kept them?'

I said yes again.

'I kept them because they were nothing in their own lives. The guerrilla—what had he but the knowledge he was going to die? Christopher and his dream of America ... All those faces just there for the taking—do you know how powerful that is, Noah?'

'Sure,' I said.

'Think you could write that feeling down, Noah?'

'Absolutely,' I said and got to my feet. 'I need a drink.' The carpet swirled and jellied as I took each step. I moved through the swirl and jelly until I reached the table of drinks and spilled whiskey into a glass.

'Want one?' I said over my shoulder.

'No,' said Belios.

He watched me walk back and slump into my chair. I stuck a cigarette into my mouth and held the lit match so close to my skin that I smelled my blood singe. I grinned at Belios.

'How do you think I live, Noah?'

'Your work? The kids chip in?'

Belios shook his head. 'I live because of what I want.'

I saluted him with my near-empty drink.

Belios leaned closer. 'You ... Noah ... you want to be me. That's a parasite's dream. That's all you have inside you. You live on that and you'll amount to nothing. Life is easy once you know your place. The parasite ... you, and the pioneer ... me. Now do you understand why you would fail? Medb is always right about the things she sees in people. You have nothing inside you that can describe me. All those exclamation points! "Africa" in capital letters. Every old cliché in your vocabulary ...'

'You're telling me I'm crap?'

'Exactly.'

I leaned down to set my glass on the fireplace and to hide my face. Pain from my head lodged behind my ears and jaw. I was fucked for a comeback and so I laughed instead. I forced my mouth open to let the sound out and then I straightened up.

'Hey old man,' I said.

Belios looked at me.

'I'm the last useable thing in your life, William.' I nodded in the general direction of where he had hidden my cigarettes. 'Give me one,' I said.

Belios stuck his fingers into the box and dragged a couple out. He nudged one across his lap at me.

'Remember Stephen Bankes?' I said into my exhaled smoke. I saw Belios' eyes widen and I knew I scored. 'I bet the fucker barely knew you and yet ... he wrote something that ended up in *Paris-Match*. Was he a parasite too?'

'I barely remember him.'

'What sort of a face had he? One that matched his suit?'

'He wasn't much of a photographer. He liked my work and so I let him write a story.'

'And take a photograph?'

'I don't remember that either.'

Belios' throat worked against the cigarette smoke and I lowered my voice to a whisper, kept it slow and reasonable.

I leaned forward and breathed extra hard. 'You said my face didn't fit. Now ... I know what that means. It means you see something.' I shoved my arm towards the gallery wall. 'Like you saw something in them. People don't really hide their faces, do they, William? It comes out in the end. I can use words, William. I can make people see you exactly as you want them to.'

Belios kept his eyes closed. I sat back and dug my neck against the chair's back. I dug it hard in against the wood above the cushioned rim to negate the screaming shit fucking pain in my head. Sweat poured and my fists slipped their hold on the arms of the chair.

Whittle the information. That's the drill. Drop Jarlath's name. Drop Stephen Bankes' name and watch the eyes. Drop Medb's name. Drop Evelyn's.

I reached down for my glass and realized it was empty. Belios nodded to himself. I thought he was falling asleep and that pissed me off. I dropped the glass. It shattered and spat into the fire. Belios opened his eyes. He looked right through me. I smiled.

'Belios,' I said. 'Belios,' I repeated.

Belios looked at me.

'I can do this, William. I'm exactly what you need.'

How many times had I made that promise and every time, it was perfect. I used to love watching the people I wrote stories about in those big colour picture books. I watched them preen for the camera, learn some memory just right for the interview and pass my name onto the next. See this guy? He can make your life mean something to somebody. He can make it perfect.

Belios smiled and I wondered about the best kind of manoeuvre towards the whiskey when Belios reminded me: 'I think I told you already, Noah—saving is for fools.'

William Belios had never been Irish enough. His name had made sure of that. It was strange and his face was strange. Too blond, too narrow, almost handsome but ugly when you get close.

'You liked that?'

'Of course. It meant I was different. It meant my face said something and it made me want more.'

William's mother, Angela, had never been anyone you could call different. She had the same wide face seen on many shop-girls up from the country. Her saving graces were that she was tall, had round brown eyes and surprisingly white straight teeth. She also read books. Every Thursday was her afternoon off and she'd appear at the National Library. William's father, Peter Belios, worked there. Half-English, half something else.

'What else?'

'He used to say Norwegian. He spoke with an accent. He too was tall. He wore a moustache and was an amateur expert on exploration and he would study my mother each Thursday afternoon. She came without fail. She was obsessed with books. She despised most romances but harboured an insane love for many saints. My father knew one important truth: love for a saint is easily commandeered. He made her love him.'

'How?'

'How do you make another love you, Noah? You become what they want. My father made my mother love him. He became her saint and they married when she became pregnant.'

Peter Belios passed himself off as a historian and an explorer. He also had blond hair and a narrow, long face.

'Perfect for worship,' said Belios. 'He also loved books and he filled a middle-sized house with them. He uprooted the tiles in the hallway and put in new ones from Morocco. Quite blue and glittering when the sun caught them.'

'All this on a library assistant's pay?'

'My father had many secrets. My mother had very few. Tell me, Noah, who had the more power there?'

They had rare dinner guests, never Irish: an American who dealt in nude statues, a card player from Sydney, an illusionist from London's East-End, a photographer from Bolivia.

'A photographer?'

'Ah, now your mind is working, Noah—a photographer from Bolivia and the start of things, how the seed was planted and so forth. Maybe it was. I don't really remember. He was a small man— more Indian than anything else. My mother loved his eyes. They were glossy brown, she said, and I believe he was her favourite.'

'Favourite what?'

'She'd come alive in a different way once he entered the room. I noticed it even if my father ignored it. The Bolivian was small, had gentle movements, and was very circumspect.'

'Did he photograph her?'

'I believe he fucked her.'

'You believe?'

'Actually, I saw.'

It was a Friday night, the sort of mid-summer evening Angela adored and she would leave one window open at night to catch the fragrance from the garden. William was thirteen and even he was delighted at how graceful his mother appeared. Tall, with her round brown eyes watching her husband's guests as they listened to him outline his travels throughout North Africa, then Afghanistan, the Black Sea, perhaps even Moscow.

Angela was used to these stories. She smiled across at the Bolivian photographer and promised to show him the garden. After coffee she led him to the garden, lit up only as far as the lights from the dining room would allow. Angela and the photographer stopped just at the edge of the light and William watched from the open window.

He glanced behind to see his father deep in conversation with the American and they were smoking the American's gift of cigars. William wanted his father to look up and see his son at the window. His father did look up. A glance away from the American and across to his son. A raised eyebrow and a smile. William wanted something more. He wanted his father to get up and walk to the window, look out and see, just on the edge of the light, the photographer's fingers brush over Angela's right hand.

His father did nothing but return to the American's story and William watched his mother melt into the garden with the man.

'You followed them?'

'Of course. I took off my shoes and slipped out the back door.'

William was never afraid of the dark. He knew that a strong smell of honeysuckle meant he was near the wall on the right side of the garden. He held out his hand as if he could touch the flower's thick odour. His mother's favourite flower.

William stood very still and listened to the dark. His toes dug into the night-damp grass as he concentrated on what he could hear. He heard the slow calling moan of his mother. He heard the Bolivian's grunts. He heard each moan and grunt slap together in the cool, honeysuckled air.

William walked in a half-circle. He watched their bodies as his eyes grew used to the dark. His mother's white full-fleshed arm gripping the photographer's brown back. Her thighs hooked about his waist and one of his arms braced on the wall behind them.

William came in his pants.

His mother opened her eyes.

'Did she see you?'

'I like to think she did.'

'Then what happened?'

William went back to the dining-room. Peter was still at the table and had dribbled salt onto the tablecloth to map out a mountain range. He glanced up at his son, dismissed him and placed three dirty knifes one after the other to represent a mountain path.

'And this place is called what?' asked someone.

'The Takla Makan,' said Peter. 'To paraphrase the translation—it means "The Place You Enter and Never Leave". People have disappeared there.'

'Except for you,' said Angela as she came through the dining-room doors on her own and smelling of the garden. She fanned her face with a white handkerchief.

'Except for me,' agreed Peter.

Angela laughed at the audience round her husband. 'He has such stories.' She poured sherry into a glass and sat down on an antique green velvet sofa. The Australian card-player rolled a small table on its legs to where she sat and announced they should play a game. The London illusionist watched from the dining-table.

'Careful,' he warned Angela. 'Aussies are slippery characters.'

Angela glanced across at him and then at Peter, who shrugged, so Angela played cards with the Australian while William sat under the window. The Bolivian photographer took his time coming back into the room and when he did Angela lifted her face and gave him her usual smile so no one noticed anything. The photographer sat down at the table, directed his attention to the knives on the table and listened to Peter's story.

'Did Peter suspect?'

'I don't know.'

'That Takla Makan story ... is that true?'

'My father often told it.'

'Courtesy of the library?'

'Perhaps.'

'What happened to the Bolivian photographer?'

'He left. My parents continued with their lives.'

'Then what happened?'

William had his fourteenth birthday followed by his fifteenth and things seemed the same except that his mind had begun to play tricks on him.

'Or perhaps it was my heart.'

His mind told him that yes, this is the table you are touching; this is your mother's face in front of you and those are your father's footsteps you hear. That is his voice and that is your mother's face turning from her book to greet him. That is how she smiles; that is how he kisses her and it was all as if it was a drama played behind a glass wall, which William had no compulsion to join.

He felt nothing. He knew that if he touched the tablecloth, his brain would tell him what he needed to know. It was blue, had a shiny, smooth quality and a gold-lace effect along its edge. William knew how to feel the cloth. He knew what he should feel as he rubbed it between his fingertips.

He knew if he kissed his mother's cheek then his lips would touch the wrinkles growing from her mouth. He would even smell her breath. He knew that if he stood close enough to his father, he would almost touch him. Yet William felt nothing.

'How do you explain that, Noah?'

'I don't know how. Maybe it had something to do with you being a teenager.'

'Do you believe in practicalities, Noah?'

'Sure.'

'Who is useful, who is not ... who can be loved, who cannot?'

'To a degree, yeah.'

Then William fell in love.

His first meeting with Katya Dressler had been romantic in his eyes. However, she had been afraid. She had large, European, doll-shaped eyes but her skin was yellow. She spilled her coffee as he passed by her table in the café and he moved fast to help her clean it up. He applauded himself at how solicitous he sounded, how decent, and he mopped up the spillage with his own handkerchief just so she would notice.

She did. She exclaimed that he was ruining it and her accent made him look right at her. She didn't appreciate that. She shut her gaze down towards the table and her fingers sidled out to reach her purse.

William picked it up, wiped underneath it and placed it down again but this time it was further away and she didn't reach for it. William sat opposite her and nodded across to a waitress who sauntered over and took his order for two coffees. 'Would you like a cake?' he asked Katya.

She shook her head but William ordered one anyway. Katya did not once touch her purse but William knew she was watching it from the corner of her eyes. He could hear her breathing and he noticed the bright silk scarf around her neck.

He used that to open the conversation. 'A beautiful scarf,' he said.

She nodded and nearly lifted her head.

William leaned in and said: 'Perhaps I could look at your face.'

The waitress arrived with the coffees and a cream slice. William cut it in half and then nudged the jug of milk towards Katya.

She picked it up and poured milk into her coffee. William hummed something under his breath, some music he had heard from some film. He tried to look harmless. He chatted about his medical studies.

Katya looked at him.

'Was she beautiful?'

'Yes.'

'Katya Dressler sounds German.'

'Her parents were.'

'Something to do with the war?'

'Clever Noah. I once asked her if she was Jewish and she said no. I loved her air of persecution and I began to love her as well.'

'So she was useful?'

'I didn't see it that way. I believed I was in love. The glass wall disappeared. When I touched her scarf, I was touching her. I presume that is what love does. I loved her.'

'What happened?'

'The glass wall came back.'

'Just like that?'

'It took its time but it reappeared. Do you know what it is like to love someone who is useless?'

'No, I don't.'

'Their vulnerability conjures up love. It makes you believe that what you feel is real. It smothers everything else until there is nothing left of what you used to be. You become what they want.'

'Which was?'

'A saviour. Only I was one of several. She turned out to be a whore.'

Katya Dressler was found dead half-naked in her digs. William's name was found in a notebook along with dates and times. The police called to his parents' door and his mother sat silent in court as they read out Katya's name and the manner of her death. William's father swore that his son was innocent.

'And were you?'

'Of course. They found someone else.'

'What happened then?'

'I entered the Church.'

The Church filled William with a hard, sick joy.

'Know what I decided at that moment, Noah?'

'What?'

'I decided that was power.'

'MORNING. Didn't you sleep?' said Karen from behind my chair.

'I've been working,' I answered. I pushed back from the desk expecting her to sit on my lap but Karen sat on the desk instead. Her face was early morning blank.

'You smell of warm bed,' I told her and touched her knee. She slipped it sideways out of my reach.

'What's up?' I said.

'Nothing,' she glanced down at my work. I moved forward to shift her aside and picked up my pen but she was too quick and grabbed the pages.

'Chapter one, I presume?'

'Give it back, Karen.'

'Oh … am I interrupting the genius at work?'

I sat back, kept my eye on the pages. All Belios' words, all my words scribbled into a pattern of paragraph and dialogue.

'Fine. Read it,' I said aloud.

Karen flicked through the pages first. 'A whole night's work?'

'Yeah.'

'And is this the beginning?'

'Yeah.'

'This is the first sentence?'

'Yeah.'

'Are you sure this should be the first sentence?'

'That's the one.'

While she read I kept my eyes on the dictaphone half-concealed under my red file.

Karen read the title out loud. '"Belios". Just that? Nothing added on … like "The life of a photographer" or "explorer" or whatever the fuck he was?'

'Just the way it is, Karen.'

She handed the pages back. 'Is it a bloody saga you're after?'

I held the pages between my palms. 'It's his life. It's how he lived it. You look at what made someone into who they are and it's like with anything else, you have to go back to the parents.'

'And you believe it?'

'Why should he lie?'

I placed the pages into my red file and sealed it. 'Money isn't the issue, Karen.'

'Bullshit. You've always done it for money … and the parties. You've done it for *The Late Late Show* and God knows who and what else and like me you've fucked the critics so why do it different now? You seem to forget that this lot aren't a bit famous and no one gives a toss.'

'It's a good story.'

'No, it bloody isn't. They're just like any other family that needs therapy to exorcise their shit! This isn't going to make money, Noah, and it isn't going to win you prizes … and it isn't healthy.'

'Meaning?'

'Ask your psychiatrist. I bet she can explain it.'

I lounged back into the chair and looked Karen up and down. She acted bored and shivered for effect.

'You look pretty,' I told her. I nodded at my night's work. 'So it's crap?'

'If I were you, I'd forget the whole thing.'

'I can't.'

'No one is going to care about a washed-up foreign photographer in Oughterard. So what? Who cares? Write about the people we are used to. That's what you are good at.'

'My "hatchet-jobs" according to you.'

'They're popular, Noah. They're entertaining. I'm sorry we ever came to this place. I should have put my foot down. I grew out of having heroes a long time ago. So should you.'

Karen nuzzled my ear then drew back. 'What the fuck happened to you?'

'I fell in the bathroom. Whacked my skull off the tiles.'

'Jesus!'

'I'm fine. I'm just fine, Karen. Don't touch anything.'

She pulled back. I smiled and her eyes narrowed, then she straddled my lap. She placed her hands above mine and said in a sweet, just-right voice.

'I miss our Sunday mornings.'

'It's not even Sunday.'

'You know what I mean, Noah. I miss the way we are. Let's go back home.'

'Soon,' I said.

'Great.' Karen swung off me and marched over to her suitcase. 'I know what you want. Me to leave, you to stay …' She rifled through her suitcase then sat back on her heels. 'I've run out of towels. I don't trust theirs. Have you extra?'

'Check my bag.'

Karen found one and snapped out its folds and said: 'You're out of your depth with this one, Noah. Just give it up.'

'I don't want to.'

Karen stood in the middle of the room and stared at me. She should still be beautiful to me in some way, I thought, and I was too used to her not to want to fuck her sometimes. Standing there, she was like a minor marble statue, very white in her cream slip with her child's face.

'Maybe I'll photograph you,' I offered. I jerked my head towards my side of the bed. 'The camera should be on the floor.'

'Noah …'

'Come on, just for me. I'm writing this the "Method" way. To know a photographer is to be one.'

Karen thought for a couple of seconds, then found the camera and lobbed it over to me. I stood up and motioned her back to the middle of the room then ordered her to turn. Her face was so white and beautiful and her lips seemed redder in the morning light. I told her to hold her head just so. I told her she reminded me of the first time we met and all the time I moved the lens closer to her face. What was I looking for? I don't fucking know.

My hands shook and Karen blurred in the lens. Fuck, went my head. Fuck, went my fingers. Fuck, went my eyes. I shut them. I breathed hard. I was afraid to see. I was afraid I'd catch just her ordinary face—the same one I tried not to see anymore.

I was aware of how quiet she was and how she stood still with a side stance guaranteed to make her look good. I saw how she watched me step even closer so that at some point she knew it wasn't a full body photograph but a portrait. At the second of her realization, I looked for signs I could catch. They came like slow shadow. She bit her lips as she stared into the lens. She fingered the hair at her temples. She glanced bird-like between my hands and the camera.

I lifted the camera and looked through the lens. In this light, Karen shone and I didn't want to breathe. I wanted it all to be holy. To have something real in the camera, something to prove to me that I was right, that I could do this, that I could do what Belios once did.

I pressed the button and the picture was taken. It took me seconds to lower the camera from my face. Karen raised her eyebrows and for something to do, I wrapped the camera's strap around my wrist and said, 'Finito.'

'About fucking time,' said Karen. She stooped to grab the towel and slung it over her shoulder. 'Thank Christ you don't do that for a living. I was bored rigid.'

'You didn't look it,' I called after her as she went into the bathroom. I stood by the doorway and grinned in at her as she stepped out of her slip, ready for the shower. She picked up the soap from the sink, then glanced at me.

'Really? Then how did I look?'

'Scared,' I said.

5

B REAKFAST WAS half-eaten by the time Karen and I arrived downstairs. Conversation died and Aoife smiled at me as we sat down so I smiled back. Medb was seated opposite me and Jarlath sat with his porridge at the head of the table.

'How did you sleep?' asked Aoife with her happy smile.

Karen answered for us: 'Fine. Noah worked too hard though. Wrote all night just to make your father look good on paper.'

Medb's glance slid over my face, across Karen's, then back onto a plate of brown bread.

'Making good progress, are you?' she said.

'Some.'

All three additions in front of me and I was ready to play. Jarlath mostly on side, Aoife with her too-happy smile and Medb ... I remembered how I felt when she looked at me in the pub, how I felt when I was in her sights. I lifted the coffee-pot: 'Anyone?' then as I poured, I said, 'Karen tells me you're a shit-hot illustrator, Medb.'

I put the coffee-pot back down. 'But I think you frightened her.'

'I didn't say that!'

'She destroyed it, Medb. Real mark of the philistine, wouldn't you say? Burnt to a crisp in the sink.'

'I can't look at Medb's work,' Aoife said. 'Jarlath tried to do her publicity once but it didn't work because he couldn't understand it.'

'A drawing is a drawing,' I said.

'Well, that's wrong actually,' continued Aoife. 'He could understand it. I mean, it's easy to understand what she draws; it's what she paints that's a bit weird.'

'Aoife can't appreciate them,' Medb said.

'I don't want to appreciate them,' Aoife said.

Medb smiled just a little and looked more at Karen than at me. 'Aoife likes things to mean something to her.'

'Nothing wrong with that,' I said.

'Why did you burn it?' Medb asked Karen.

'Not my cup of tea at all,' Karen replied. 'It was too ... studied.'

'You mean you weren't naked?' said Jarlath.

'I was not! I was just myself.'

'So what's weird about your paintings?' I said to Medb.

'I draw erotic pictures,' she said.

'Pornography?' This from Karen.

'In some circles it's art,' replied Medb.

I turned and looked Karen up and down. 'Why didn't you take your clothes off? I could have framed it; could have hung it above the mantlepiece and made you the centre of every conversation and ...' I looked back at my audience. 'If Medb's any good ... we could make her famous, couldn't we, Karen?'

'No matter how well I've trained him,' Karen said, 'he's still a prick at breakfast-time.'

'Hey Medb,' I said. I leaned in over the table and I knew just how I looked, like a bulldozer made flesh. Medb was the one to watch. Medb was the one I wanted to catch. Her eyes were calm but I heard the breath pull back in her throat.

'You see, Medb, your dad's biography wouldn't be worth the paper it was written on if it was just another story. As Karen so brilliantly put it earlier this morning ... who's interested in another fucked-up Irish family? Only ... there are always reasons to write about another fucked-up Irish family and I'd be a fool if I didn't mix them in.'

I had their attention now so I played it for all I was worth. I ignored Karen's deliberate reach for the coffee-pot that hampered my view of Medb—instead I smiled at Jarlath and then at Aoife.

'Hey Aoife,' I said. Aoife, the other addition. Aoife, the sister with a smile. Aoife, who loves her daddy.

I held up my hand and said, 'Three kids. Three personalities ... you, Jarlath and Medb. A very interesting family complete with dead mother and a father rotting away upstairs with cancer. So already there must be fascinating reasons that the three of you are still here and nowhere else. Do you see what I'm getting at, Aoife?'

Aoife didn't answer.

'Well maybe Medb can see,' I said.

Medb said nothing so I glanced over at Jarlath, who kept eating.

'It couldn't be simpler,' I said. 'Aoife, you tell me what you remember and I write it down. I write it down such a way that it tells your father's story with you inside it. See what I mean?'

'Maybe Aoife can't be bothered,' said Karen. 'You know, maybe she can't be arsed. Maybe she's listening to you right now and thinking, What a fucking fraud.'

Medb's word. Medb's word hung in the air.

I counted to five. Karen didn't move. Jarlath made some noise in his throat and Aoife pushed away her bowl from in front of her. I couldn't look at Medb so I kept my eyes on Aoife.

'It goes like this, Aoife. Everyone fits into certain stereotypes. I mean, what story doesn't rely on them but it's what's underneath that matters. That's where the meat is. "Middle child syndrome", Aoife, can be tough. Married once; it didn't work out. The pregnancy didn't work out either. I mean, who hasn't experienced things like that?'

I saw Medb lift one hand and then press it down on top of Aoife's. But Aoife slid her hand from under it.

I forgot Karen beside me. I forgot Jarlath after I took one quick glance at his pale face. I even forgot Medb. I smelled gold instead. Had I planned it this way? I couldn't remember. I knew I had used the same patter on others. Peeled back their scabs just enough to make them wince but never enough to make them run for cover.

'What if there was a story behind the middle child? What if it was a secret? Secrets don't just appear, do they? They could have roots—great big ones that could go all the way back to your mom in Africa.'

'What are you on about, Noah?' said Karen.

I wanted something to change in Aoife's face. But there was nothing I could use. She buttered the remainder of her toast and spread on some marmalade.

'Try me,' said Medb.

I looked at Medb and I said: 'Jarlath tells me you don't think I've the balls.'

I looked at Medb and willed the shake out of my hands. I willed it out of my voice—exactly as I had done with Belios.

'Hey Medb,' I said.

Those eyes of hers slung into me. 'Hey Medb.' Just to say it again. I looked at the line of her body against the light of the window behind her, the garden beyond that, the fucking brilliant summer morning, and I felt that cold hate in my stomach, just like it is for Claire.

'Hey Medb,' I said as my mobile rang. I answered it then handed it to Karen.

'Anita,' I said.

'Yeah?' Karen said into the phone. 'It's turned off, Anita. Well … that's what you do when you're in the arsehole of nowhere; you communicate with nature instead. Did you get our postcard? Jesus, the fucking post. Yeah well, it's from both of us … yeah … I don't know … soon. Fuck off, Anita, you're a great one for the guilt. Yeah, bye.'

As Karen had spoken into the mobile, I saw the hope of diversion in Medb's face and I wanted to ruin it. 'I want to photograph you all.'

'You?' said Medb.

'Me,' I said.

'In other words, an amateur,' said Karen.

'Can't have the book without the faces to go with it,' I said.

Jarlath shrugged. 'Fine as far as I'm concerned.'

'Will they be in colour?' said Aoife.

'I prefer black and white,' I said.

I knew Medb was watching me but I kept my smile on Aoife as she stood up from her chair and walked fast out of the room. We heard her footsteps across the hall, then up the stairs.

'Hey Karen, want to swim?' offered Jarlath.

'Absolutely not.'

'Want to sight-see?'

'What's to see? Tourists?'

'Karen, I want to chat with Medb.'

'Really, Noah?'

'Karen … let Jarlath surprise you.'

Just a few seconds and she made up her mind. 'Maybe I'll do that.'

Jarlath waited at the door for Karen while she leaned down and kissed my cheek.

In the lowest whisper she could manage, she said: 'Why don't you look at me and pretend?'

I raised my face so she could kiss my mouth. Her hand squeezed my shoulder and I felt her shiver. I moved my head away. She straightened up and left the room.

'She must love you,' said Medb as her brother shut the door.

'She does.'

'Do you love her?'

'Not really,' I said.

'Yet you're with her.'

'You believe in fairy tales, Medb?'

Medb shook her head. 'I read every one of your letters, Noah, and you've turned up like something on heat. So … no, I don't believe in fairy-tales. I believe in motives.'

'Your father is telling me his story.'

'And you believe it?'

'Why not?'

'Oh, the priest part is true. The fact we were born means we are his. The fact that we live here means we left Africa. What's in between all that is his version.'

'That's why I want yours.'

'That's not his story.'

'I want your photograph in my book. I want it all in my book.'

'And what does he want?'

'The same thing that everyone I write about does. Fame.'

'He doesn't need that.'

'Maybe he wants forgiveness.'

'For what?'

'Well, there's always Katya Dressler.'

'Who?'

I watched her face and decided she could be a very good actress if she wanted to. 'Some whore he once loved,' I said to mess up the blankness in her face. 'There's even a suggestion he was nearly done for her murder.'

The blankness switched off. Bullseye. I smiled: 'Maybe that's where the forgiveness comes in but who the fuck knows. Maybe he just wants to be remembered. Greatest fantasy of the dying is to be remembered.'

Lily in her bed and her flesh shrivelling to her bones. The smell of her breath against my mouth and the lonely fucker of a husband in the chair, his hands clawed into his jumper as if to claw out his heart.

Somehow I knew Belios wasn't after that kind of remembrance.

'What about you?' I whispered.

She glanced at me. 'What?'

'You draw my girlfriend just to get me to notice you. You despise what I do but you know my work and you've read every letter.'

Seconds passed but I could wait. I busied myself with a little ritual. Three seconds from her face to stare at the painting hung beside the patio door, five seconds on her face, three directed onto the garden, then back again.

'What did you promise my father?' Medb said.

'I promised I'd write down everything.'

She pushed back her chair.

'Don't go,' I said.

'I've work to do,' she said.

'Oh yeah, the pornography. Daddy knows what buys his bread and jam?'

'He knows what I do.'

I stood up. 'Maybe he's ashamed, Medb. All that rich photography of his filtered down to nothing but pictures to wank to. Come on, Medb. Got to admit you're the disappointment. Jarlath's boring but at least he's doing the community some good and Aoife's the one Daddy depends on ... how many dots do you think I'll need, Medb?'

She stood up but I could still see goosebumps on the skin at her collarbone. If I had the guts, I would have kissed her then.

'Maybe you would like to be as useful as Aoife is?' I said.

She stepped back and made for the door but I moved fast and blocked her before she reached it. Even then she seemed barely afraid. I kept moving her until her back was almost against the wall. Her eyes flicked to the door.

Karen and I had played this game until it bored us. How many versions of predatory bastard and innocent prey can there be? Karen was right—things were too easy once they followed a pattern—but with Medb in front of me, things developed an acid flavour again like lemon on the tongue and I felt the slow juicy burn of anger in my gut. The doll-bitch's face was beneath mine and I couldn't see her eyes. Maybe they hated me back. I pressed myself forward and her face came up.

The first thing any camera buff tells you: eyes never fucking lie. Use any light you want, invent any background you like, go through the motions, but your eyes are the way God made them. So saith Belios.

Medb's eyes were narrow, curved and grey in the light and looking into mine. Hate shifted from my gut upwards until my lungs scorched with it. I could see the wall. I could see her body. I could also remember how Karen would act out the whole episode, how she'd wrap her legs and where she'd place her mouth.

Medb didn't move back but I could smell her fear. I looked at her. Fuck her. Fuck her. Move your hand, just your hand, place it on her stomach and push her back so that the wall holds you both. How much pain would she need? I tried to gauge by her face, just seconds before I would touch her again and that made me think of her hands and where she'd decide to put them on me.

I looked at her hands. They hung straight. The cuffs of her blouse were long and stained with dried-on paint. There was paint on her hand just above her thumb. I looked closer and realized it was a blood blister. I took her hand in mine and pressed hard on the blister. She breathed in the pain. We looked at each other. I pressed harder and the pain shot into her face. I pushed my thumb and felt a scabbed thread-like scar that travelled beyond her wrist. She let my thumb follow just so far before she yanked her hand free, pushed me aside and then she was gone.

God made eyes.

I wrote that sentence down. I sat in the bedroom transcribing his words onto pages and made them mine. I had a fantasy in my head: the reader being me; the reader desiring this life as his. Isn't that what biography is, Noah? All those fools wanting a life to worship, a life to feed on.

I propped up Belios' photograph against a book. It would be good for the cover. Ex-priest photographer-explorer with secrets. The sun was high in the sky when the photograph was taken and although there was a large house behind him, its windows weren't close enough to reflect the photographer. Evelyn, maybe.

Maybe she believed a photograph meant your soul. It made sense and it would look good on paper. That kind of version would sell.

I dialled Jerry's mobile. No answer. I rang his office.

'He's not in,' said his P.A.

'To me or to anyone, Christine?'

'Who are you?'

'Noah Gilmore.'

'Try his mobile,' she said.

'Maybe I could leave a message?'

'Fine, Mr Gilmore. What is it?'

'Tell him ... I have a real story. Tell him it has everything he wants. It has sex, it has death and it has mystery. Tell him I'm writing it. Tell him Claire has worked wonders and I'm actually sane ... no ... I'll rephrase that ... she says I'm normal and I have to believe her. Yeah, that's it. Tell him, as far as I can tell, the tablets are working and I look normal. Have you that written down?'

'Every word, Mr Gilmore.'

'How are you these days, Christine?'

'Busy, Mr Gilmore.'

'You sound good on the phone, Christine.'

'Goodbye, Mr Gilmore.'

I tried to get back to work so I switched on the dictaphone and listened to William Belios' voice continue with his story.

'Have you ever thought how necessary suffering is, Noah?'

'No.'

'Forget the Jesuits. Forget the Bible. Forget the prayers. Forget the orgasmic visions of the saints. That's not suffering. That's Day-Glo religion. Reel in the useless and feed them all the salvation they can gorge on.'

'Oh, so you're a guru now, are you?'

'God made our eyes, Noah, but our suffering is our own.' William tapped the corner of his eye. 'Everything you see in those photographs is man-made and we can't live without it.'

'That's profound shit, William.'

William's laugh on the tape was too real and I switched it off. I turned in my chair but the room was still empty. It was almost twelve. A whole fucking day ahead of me. I noticed the camera where I had left it and during the long seconds I stared at it, I decided no more writing. Get the camera out and put Aoife in front of it. Then Jarlath. Then Medb. Medb for last. Medb with her hair down and some skin showing. Take the goddamn pictures. Write down the shit. Screw the old bastard down.

'Isn't that what they say?' said Claire. 'Write it all down?'

This was my ninth week at her office. She put up with my smoking and her pretty knees peeped from beneath her skirt.

'A diary,' she suggested.

'For fuck's sake,' I said. 'I'm not that into myself.'

'It helps.'

'Well, you're the psychiatrist. So, any special notebook? Any just-the-perfect-coloured pen? Where are the tools, Claire?'

'All this anger is pointless. You're not putting it anywhere. It's obvious you despise your life. And what do you do for a living? You write about other people's lives.'

I tried to stare her down but perfect, analytical Claire was having none of that. She smiled and suggested I find the nearest newsagents and buy a cheap copybook. She handed me a biro and said it was a gift.

'I'd write shit, Claire.'

Claire took off her glasses, breathed on them, snapped a tissue from its box and wiped each lens clean.

Claire put her glasses back on. She was more beautiful then. She noticed that I glanced at her knees and she coughed.

'I think you expect too much from your trauma, Noah. Freaking out in your boss's office is no clear sign of madness. It happens every day and people still turn up on a Friday for their pay cheque.'

'How the fuck did you ever graduate, Claire? I told you I have dreams. My hands shake. I hurt Karen. She tells me it's fine with her. She tells me she wants it. Tell me what fucking feminist would look me in the eyes and say, "Don't worry. It's a normal state of affairs." I mean how the fuck will writing all this down make everything okay?'

I was sweating. My hands shook and I had dropped the pen. I didn't bother to pick it up. Moments passed and we both watched the clock.

'What if there was something else, Claire?'

'Like what?'

'What if the dreams were more?'

'You mean——if they were real?'

'If I acted them out.'

'You can't, Noah. The body is flooded with inhibitors while you sleep. And you are not a sleepwalker, are you?'

'Couldn't I make them real? What if I wanted to make them real?'

Claire stared at me. 'Then I couldn't help you anymore. I wouldn't be enough for you.'

I smiled. 'So, it's just as well that they are dreams then, isn't it?'

'What do your dreams tell you, Noah?'

I shrugged. 'Nothing much. Just shit from the day all mixed up into the bogeyman.' I smiled at her. 'Hey, I know the difference. Dreams aren't real.'

She wrote me another prescription and marked our next appointment in her diary. That night Karen and I went out and I sat in the club and watched her dance. She put up with my mood and bit my ear when she kissed me between dances. We fucked once in the toilets just like we used to and afterwards she lifted her hair so I could kiss her neck. The strap broke on one of her sandals and she held onto me as she tried to fix it. She gave up after a few seconds and I carried her out.

In the cab on the way home she looked out of the window and said something.

'What?'

She turned and smiled at me. 'You know I'm drunk, Noah.'

'Sure.'

'That was sweet back there,' she said.

'The toilets?'

'Like we meant it. I love it when we do it like that. It's always better when it's like that.' She looked out the window again while I studied the taxi-driver's ID on the dashboard. Karen turned from the window and touched my arm. She was crying. She put her face into my jacket until she stopped. Then she sat back, fixed her hair and said: 'It's always better when I'm drunk.'

I held her hand and kissed it but when we got home, I locked myself into the bathroom, had a shower, took one pill, two, three and four and my face smiled in the mirror. Hey Noah, it said to me. Hey Noah, how the fuck have you managed so long?

6

G OD MADE EYES.
The first time William Belios held a camerwas after an execution. He'd been a priest for five years and its power had become
boring. He was rotting in his own hell in the Nigerian bush.

A young priest from Tullamore had joined him there. Full of ideas
and determined to be modern no matter how dangerous it sounded.

'Liberal theology,' announced the young priest as he and William
walked towards the church to hear confession. 'Do you understand it?'

William stopped and said: 'No.'

He kept the young priest out in the midday sun and made him
explain. The Tullamore priest had pink-white skin that roasted red.

'Missions,' said the Tullamore priest. 'They don't work if we just
have God. We need something else. We need human understanding.
Not just what the Church interprets but also the good humanity in
all of us and … and … a respect for the other side of things.'

'Which is?'

The young priest plucked his shirt free from his trousers and
wiped the sweat from his face.

'Father, I think we should go inside.' He smiled and tried a joke,
'All the sinners are waiting on their knees.'

'Not just yet,' said William. He was enjoying himself. Time enough for those faces behind the grille. Time enough for those sins so normal in everyday life and abolished in the Church. Time enough for the litany of useless prayers.

William pursed his mouth as if he was thinking hard about the Tullamore priest's handy theory of new religion while the young priest kept wiping his neck. 'The good and bad. They fit together.' He locked his hands into prayer position all the better to demonstrate. 'And sometimes bad needs to be met head-on. Saying Mass isn't always enough.' He grinned at William and gestured towards the church. His feet moved two steps but halted when William didn't follow.

A Bishop's letter had come with this priest. It had warned William to make him a good priest, mindful of the virtue of obedience and to teach him the duties of a man of God.

William Belios was a good priest. He kept his stature intact. His Masses were well attended. The Bishop respected him and never knew that each time he held out his hand for William to kiss his ring, his seal of God's love, William held some spit behind his teeth.

'Saying Mass is never enough,' William said aloud.

The Tullamore priest nodded his head and his sweat sprinkled William's shirt. He mumbled an apology and fled to the church.

William followed him and was halfway across the compound when a young boy came running. The boy was incoherent. William shouted at the Tullamore priest to follow him and the two raced towards the south end of the compound to where the school's staff had their homes.

There was a crowd outside one house and blood spilled down its front door veranda. 'Holy Christ,' whispered the Tullamore priest.

The blood was thick in places, hardening up in the heat. Spectators slipped and drew blood skid-marks. There were shouts and whispers and a white arm had flopped downwards towards the veranda's steps.

'Father,' said a young man to William's right.

William knew the young man's name but he couldn't remember it; the picture of the white arm filled his mind.

'Father.' The young man tugged at Belios' shoulder.

'Joseph?' said Belios.

Joseph shoved at people to move back and steered William towards the body that sprawled out of the front door. William recognized him—Declan Meeney, a young mathematics teacher, very popular and married to a local girl. The crowd moved back into a wider circle to allow William to crouch down and look at the body. Declan Meeney's eyes were gone.

Joseph crouched down and his hand hovered above Declan's butchered face. He made a low, guttural scream inside his throat, 'Ah-ah-ah-ah.'

'Why?' said William.

Joseph shrugged. 'She got tired maybe,' he said.

William glanced into the room beyond the front door. 'Is she gone?'

Joseph shook his head, then shrugged his shoulders. He cast a quick glance about the floor beneath him before sitting down on a bloodless patch.

William heard a police siren and he stood up to watch the car zoom in and park a few feet away. The police dispersed the crowd to a ring outside the house's fence. The officer in charge recognized William and bowed his head in greeting.

'Bad business,' said the Tullamore priest.

The officer circled the body and sucked his teeth when he saw the sightless holes. 'Bad business,' he mimicked the priest.

'White man, black woman—doesn't always work,' said William.

The officer looked up with an easy smile. 'Hearsay, Father, until we find her.'

The officer was Ibo and from Lagos. British-educated—he wore a suit and tie when he wasn't in uniform and he attended the dances in the hotel in town. He stood up and took off his cap to fan his face, then smiled at William.

'Well, Father ... don't you have to say something?'

William motioned to the Tullamore priest.

'But I need ...' he objected.

'Never mind what you need,' said William. 'Just say the prayers.'

He kneeled down and glanced up when William didn't follow suit. William listened to the prayers of the dead while he studied the body in front of him. He hadn't really known Declan Meeney but he knew his story.

The young teacher had fallen in love with a seventeen-year-old girl and 'went native'. They went to the market together in town and she wore up-to-date Western clothes fashioned by the local tailor and everything was just fine and wonderful until Declan Meeney became homesick.

'He wrote letters,' said the officer as he drank the whiskey William offered him later that night. 'We found replies. His family was not happy with his marriage. They said he could not come back with her.' The officer smiled into his glass, 'They do not like a black skin.'

'A fact of life for some,' said William.

The officer smiled even more. 'Me? I tell myself I have the colour God gave me and as long as I stay in my own country I am understood. But you and your kind, Father—you come here with a white man's way to deal with life.'

'Do you know what happened?'

'Yes. He was going to leave her. She begged and he wouldn't listen. He said he was leaving the house to teach a lesson and she hit him with the axe and then used a knife to take out his eyes. Do you know why she did that, Father?'

William knew but shook his head.

The officer held out his glass for more whiskey and when it was poured he laughed. 'This is where you whites think we are crazy but to us it can make sense. You kill a man and your face is the last one he sees. If you take his eyes … then no one will know.'

'Like a camera,' said William.

When he was leaving, the officer stood at the doorway looking at the night. 'Of course, we will hang her. Will you attend?'

'Was she Catholic?'

The officer shrugged. 'Perhaps—but she has stopped talking. Goodnight, Father.'

On the day of the hanging, William dressed in ordinary clothes and drove the jeep into town. He parked and locked up then walked to the hotel opposite the police headquarters. He sat on the veranda and ordered a drink. For a while, he was the only one there. Most people preferred the large fan-driven coolness of the hotel's bar but William wanted to watch the building where the woman was to be hanged.

He sat back in his chair and closed his eyes. A small breeze lifted from somewhere and reached his face. It cooled the sweat on his neck and he felt the tickling of flies against his leg. He moved his leg and they buzzed into the air, buzzed closer to his ear and he swatted them away with his eyes still closed.

'All right if I sit here?' said a woman's voice.

William opened his eyes. A young woman dressed in a blue cotton skirt and a white shirt stood in front of him. He nodded and sat straight. She sat down and smiled before she took a quick sip of her drink. Her red hair lay in sweat tails about her neck. She jerked her head back towards the bar.

'They're all talk about it in there,' she said in an Irish accent. 'They think we should march against police headquarters and demand the hanging postponed.' She tried to laugh. 'They think that's humane. They don't think she had a proper trial. No one saw her kill him but they kept after her until she dug up his eyeballs. Most of them in there consider the whole thing far too quick. They want to be inside taking notes. They want to drink it all in.'

'What do you think?' said William.

The young woman shrugged. 'This is Africa. In France, maybe the girl would have got off: *crime passionel*. In Ireland, she could have pleaded insanity. Here, they just think she has the devil inside her and so she gets hung.'

'It's a savage world,' said William.

'Don't give me that,' said the young woman. 'It's just bloody human, really. The whole thing is too human to stomach.' She smiled. 'I'm Evelyn Flaherty. You?'

'William Belios.'

'Teacher?'

'No. Priest.'

'Jesus Christ,' laughed Evelyn. She brushed sweat away from her forehead, then gripped her glass. She looked shy and caught-out and got up to leave. Belios stopped her, told her to sit back down and asked her what was she doing in Africa.

'Journalist,' she smiled and held up her hands. 'It's a pretty romantic job they tell me, or at least that's what I fell for. Freelance Africa Correspondent. My job is to tell them all the stories they want to hear about little black babies. When I get home, I'm big news in the village. They expect me to be black next.'

'You must have great job satisfaction,' said William.

'Why not,' she replied. She sat back in the cane chair and plucked her blouse for coolness while her attention strayed to the large building across the street.

'Seems barbaric,' said William, following her gaze. 'Death for death. Too biblical for my liking. Too simple. Do you smoke, Evelyn?'

Evelyn shook her head and shifted to glance towards the hotel bar. She nodded at his drink.

'Want some more, Father?'

He answered vodka and lime and watched her go, still plucking her blouse with one hand and holding out her other arm to embrace the bar's fanned air. William rested his head back against his chair and listened to the veranda filling up with English, French, Italians, money-eyed Nigerians. Most people recognized him and a few faces curled with displeasure. He saluted them with a nod and watched for Evelyn's return. She took her time and for an odd reason, he didn't want her to be late. Two o'clock was the execution deadline and he wanted her here. He wanted to see her face.

He stared at her empty chair opposite him and imagined how she would sit—sideways again with her gaze turned towards police headquarters. He couldn't decide whether to look at her when the time came or to look towards the hanging compound.

He glanced up when he heard someone call out her name. Someone motioned her over but she refused and jerked her head towards William. The colleague sat down and watched Evelyn's back and legs then rolled his gaze on to William.

'Hey Evelyn? What the fuck are you reduced to?'

Evelyn mouthed 'sorry' at William as she handed him his drink. He shrugged and thanked her.

'Jesus,' marvelled Evelyn. 'A priest drinking at an execution. There's an angle for me now.'

She sat ramrod-straight in her chair and William knew she was trying hard not to be afraid. She was trying to look like everyone else but her smile flickered too much and her eyes moved from one hotel guest to another, too fast—then back again over the faces. She reached into her bag and took out a notebook and pencil. Her hand trembled as she wrote.

She glanced over at William. 'I hope you are taking in the whole atmosphere, Father. Such a fucking brilliant footnote to your Sunday sermon.'

'You're drunk,' said William.

'I am.' She flipped the notebook closed. 'What other way is there to be when the execution is behind walls and I drink rum?'

'It's not our country,' stated William.

'Yeah, good excuse as any. Next thing you'll be telling me is that God doesn't want you to get your soul dirty.'

'Maybe you feel too much,' said William.

'Because I'm a woman? Or because I'm white?'

William liked the anger in her eyes. It made her almost cry and inside him he felt the emptiness move and switch like something alive.

'I don't mean it like that. It's just not our culture. Tribal customs mixed up with law ... it's not always nice. It's just the way things are done here. Blame it on the whites if you want.'

'Oh, I do.'

Evelyn drank her rum in quick gulps. Her gaze scanned over the crowd but stopped short as a drunken man rose to his feet while tapping a spoon against his glass.

'Ladies and gentlemen!'

The talk slowed to a mumble, then absolute quiet. William did not take his eyes off Evelyn. The self-appointed master of ceremonies held up his right hand and his audience's attention swivelled towards the prison.

'Any second now,' said the drunk.

Evelyn dipped her gaze towards the table then closed her eyes. William counted the seconds it took for her to open them. She kept her eyes on her drink and William decided to ignore the spectacle and watch Evelyn instead.

From behind the prison walls came a shout, then silence and then the sick lurching sighs of all those who had waited and now wanted something more of a view—like the reality of a young woman's body hanging in hot air. Evelyn didn't raise her face until most of the spectators had returned to their drinks and the talk rose and at some tables it even turned to laughter. Evelyn picked up her drink and drank it down. Her face was very pale and her eyes bore so hard into William that he could only say the most inane thing he could think of.

'I don't have any of the answers, Evelyn.'

She was crying now. In strong, absolute silence her face was daring him to understand and the emptiness in him switched again, crawled and then retreated to somewhere in his gut.

Evelyn invited William to the morgue. The sun's heat had reached inside the cold cement-slab room, raising the temperature and the smell of the half-clothed dead girl who lay with her neck braced between two red bricks.

'Jesus,' breathed Evelyn. She opened her bag and took out a camera. She handed William her bag. He slung it about his wrist and watched as she approached the girl's body.

'Why the photograph, Evelyn?'

'Someone will pay for it,' she answered. She nodded at a guard for permission before she raised the camera, focused and began taking pictures in methodical silence and at various angles. She breathed through her nose and her sweat caused her fingers to slip and the camera fell onto the dead girl's breast.

'Fuck,' whispered Evelyn. She picked up her camera and then did a strange thing. She placed her hand where the camera had fallen, closed her eyes and mouthed a prayer. William glanced over at the guard, who stared at the opposite wall.

'Some life,' said Evelyn and buttoned up the girl's blouse. 'Aren't you supposed to say something like the last rites?'

'She wasn't Catholic.'

'That has you off the hook then.' Evelyn leaned over the girl's face and said almost to herself. 'Can you imagine all the plans she had? All the reasons to sleep with a white man and just maybe love him enough to make it worthwhile?'

'You think she loved him?'

Evelyn half-smiled. 'Who knows? She was poor so she opened her legs to the white man.' Evelyn squinted up towards the ceiling. 'Lighting is shit in here and I forgot to bring more flashes. As soon as they provide me with a real photographer, my life will be just wonderful. Tell me, Father William, how come a priest sits on a veranda, drinks vodka, waits until the execution is over and then does the one thing that all those out there were slavering to do—comes and looks at the dead black girl with the broken neck?'

'Curiosity,' explained William.

'Why don't you act like a real priest and say a prayer for her?'

Evelyn stepped back to allow him access. William took a deep breath against the stink and then noticed the bruises dinged into the dead girl's skin where she had been beaten. There were swathes of scraped skin and dried blood and the thick meaty odour made him retch. He bent over from the waist and his hand brushed the dead girl as he sought to anchor himself while he vomited colourless, vodka-flavoured bile.

He should have been used to this. A dead body can only rot and in his past he had witnessed enough funerals to hold his breath and act the priest. Blood pumped into his face and the guard shouted out but William righted himself and waved back the doctor that rushed into the room.

William stood over the dead girl's face and recited the Our Father. The girl's eyes were still open and they stared sightless into his. His gut stirred and he swallowed.

'Did you photograph her face?'

'Kind of,' said Evelyn.

'No one dug her eyes out,' he said aloud.

'That's the law for you,' said Evelyn.

William looked over at Evelyn. 'But they forgot to close them.' He held out his hand and it took seconds for her to realize that he wanted her camera. William held the camera to his eyes and the dead girl's face filled the lens. Her face had grown grotesque in the heat. Her features had widened and flattened. Her mouth had dropped open while her eyes stared dead just above the lens eyeline.

'Move her head,' ordered William and motioned the doctor forwards. 'Move the bricks. Now put something under her head and make her look at me. Fine. Now leave her.' William checked the lens, lowered it and looked at the girl's face. He moved closer, studied where his shadow fell and moved back.

'You're a photographer,' said Evelyn.

'When I was younger, I knew a photographer. He took pictures of my mother. Always wanted to know what one of these felt like.' William lobbed Evelyn's camera from one hand to the other. 'Feels good,' he said.

He lifted the camera and looked through. Now the dead girl was looking at him and he didn't want to breathe. It was the second time William was so close to a dead body. So close that he could imagine it almost alive and waiting for him. Katya had been like that. Her hands just as he remembered them, crooked and dead but only just, or at least that is how they had seemed since the day had darkened outside the window and the light in the room had not been strong enough to counter the shadows that twisted as he had twisted, looking first that way, then the other; imprinting Katya's body into his brain.

The dead girl's eyes wanted to see. Her head wanted to move, twist and look at all these eyes looking down at her. William's heart pounded. The girl was dead. He knew she was dead and yet her eyes stared up at him with all her suffering frozen inside them. William's mouth was dry and a sensation opened in his stomach as though it were ready for food. William pressed the camera shutter twice more before turning its lens upward at his own face.

'I'm in the wrong profession,' he announced.

Outside the prison, Evelyn said goodbye twice and still did not walk away. She suggested another drink. This time they sat at the bar amongst the late afternoon crowd of consulate wives and William drank as much vodka as he could to get the dead girl's smell out of his head.

'Bloody murder,' stated Evelyn. 'It's so fucking accepted here.

They'll have their drinks, some will have their dinner, go home either to the husband or upstairs to the lover. Everything is feasible. Must do your head in, Father William.'

'Call me William.'

He looked at her face and at her dark red hair. There were lines beginning at her eyes and her skin had a thirsty look, as if it needed some kind of softness just to make her like everyone else.

'Call me William,' he said again.

'What for?'

'Because I want to be your photographer.'

Evelyn laughed. 'Jesus, Father William. Your vodka is dangerous.'

'I mean it.'

'Sure you do. Look, Father. Africa can drive people mad. You look into the horizon far enough and you think you're someone else. It's actually normal here.'

Evelyn continued drinking. William waited exactly ten seconds before he heard his words come out in a rush and the blood in his body drummed, wouldn't stop drumming, made him sweat, made his words fall in thick spits and made him grab her arm so that her eyes swung at him.

'What I did in there,' he said. 'That's what I want. Do you understand? Do you know what that means? When you write in those little notebooks of yours, how does that make you feel? You scribble it all down—all that suffering you see. You spout out all your principles and where does it get you? A sleazy job and a sleazy bed with whoever is handy. Is that the life they'd like to hear about in that precious village of yours?'

William leaned his face closer to Evelyn. The smell of her sweat drove the smell of death out of his head. She tried to pull free but he gripped her harder. Her tears made her eyes greener.

She was beautiful, Noah. You must understand she was beautiful.

The emptiness twisted inside him; twisted into almost nothing when she made a low sound in her throat.

He unclasped her hand but she did not withdraw and their foreheads almost touched.

'You need a photographer,' said William.

'You know nothing about photography.'

'I know this much. No priest would do what I did. No priest would follow you into a morgue, watch you photograph a dead body, then ask to have a turn. How can I go back to saying Mass after that?'

'You're a priest. You took vows.'

'They're nothing to me.'

'This is crazy,' she said and William watched how her cheeks moved with the sound of her words. 'Madness from the sun. Go home, Father William. Bless yourself as many times as you have to and forget this whole fucking day. It's enough that a priest is curious about an execution but then to proposition me afterwards is something even the good sinners here would balk at.'

'I want to be your photographer.'

'Just like that?'

'Exactly like that.'

'You're mad,' said Evelyn and pulled her face away from his. Her gaze shifted to the bar, then to the entrance, as if pleading for someone to appear. Her fingernails tapped near silent on her chair's armrest. She bit her lips and William knew he had won. He clicked his fingers for service and ordered more drinks. He glanced down at his hands and thought of the dead girl's eyes.

The waiter came with the drinks, William Belios grabbed each one so that they sloshed over his hands. He apologized, tipped the waiter and placed Evelyn's drink in front of her.

'Want to know something?' he said. 'Something that girl knew and most people forget?'

Evelyn looked at him then, ready to hear the answer.

'God made our eyes,' said William Belios.

IT WAS a good story. The 'God made our eyes' bit made it almost perfect. A fucking cliché that made some kind of sense. Eyes don't lie, do they? Train a lens long enough and something always breaks inside. Something gives up, turns to the camera and says, Here I am. Am I not what you were always afraid of?

I got up from the desk, took a piss and went back into the bedroom. I stood and stared at the camera I had bought. I picked it up and examined the hard plastic cover with its peeling price label. I held that piece of shit in my hands and I felt nothing. I rewound the film, prised it out and snapped it into its canister. I put the camera in my inside pocket, grabbed the dictaphone and decided, fuck it. Act the part. Play the man with the mission. It's what Belios wants.

I wanted my questions answered. What made you do it, Belios? What did you see? I walked down the hallway and his words were in my head and my footsteps were too loud on the semi-carpeted wooden floor. All I fucking needed was Medb. She could have stopped me. If she would have just slipped sideways from some shadow, some corner I couldn't see, I could have been happy some-how. If that's what it's called theses days. It's what Claire would have called it: Living in the Now. Fucking Claire—I told myself—best thing I never did. I stopped three feet from Belios' door and I still expected Medb but there was nothing but the silent hallway so I knocked on the door and Aoife answered it.

'Hi,' I said and tried to get by her.

She put out her right hand level with my stomach and stopped me.

'Bad time?' I said and looked over at Belios, who was lying down on a low daybed, propped up with pillows.

'Deathbed conversations usually are,' he said.

Aoife made her way over to Belios. He shifted his leg to make room for her to sit. She leaned towards him and placed her cheek against his. Father and daughter had the look of loving tomb effigies and their silence grew into the room.

I had to breathe through my mouth again. I didn't want to look but the angle of their embracing bodies lured me. It was beautiful. It was art of some kind. And it was too real, too raw. My hands shook so I sat down. An audience of one and I waited until I could hear my own voice in my head repeating what I should say; say anything to make things a little normal, a little more suited to the sun outside the windows, to the cars I could almost hear if I concentrated hard enough.

'I brought my camera with me,' I said.

Aoife sat up and looked at me.

Belios had moved one hand from Aoife's waist to her upper

thigh. I coughed hard to give myself time to think. I took out the camera and I remembered no film but I played it for real.

'Let's have a look at your face, Aoife.'

Her face filled the lens and I tried to see into her eyes. Tried to see what could have been behind the blankness she was forcing me to see. I knew it couldn't be real. Nothing she was showing me could be real. You don't lie down with your father like that. You don't arrange a show. You don't pretend that kind of love.

Inside the lens her face was pale as a saint's. Her eyes had the wide stare of a doll's. She looked beautiful. That beauty tore into my gut and woke up my red-fuck rage. I tried to think of the words. Tried to haul them out so I could fling them at her and rip her eyes open to whatever was behind them and so I said: 'What's it like to lose a baby, Aoife?'

Her saint's face curdled with shock at my words. But I kept the lens on her eyes, willed my words to invade.

One tear from her left eye and the camera followed its track to her lips, then the lens went back to her eyes and there I saw they were wide with colour and pain. The pale saint's face was butchered with it. Aoife had the live face of suffering and her eyes made me feel as if I could reach and touch her. Put my face against hers and keep her like that: stripped for the lens, raw and real.

And so I clicked the camera. And nothing happened.

I had forgotten that there was no film. I turned the camera to face me and I knew what I had seen. Knew it in my gut yet I didn't have the balls to look back up at Aoife without the camera.

I heard her move, stand up and walk out of the room.

After long seconds I looked over at Belios. 'Bravo,' he said. He opened his hands like a priest of old and I, like the desperate fuck I was, considered it some kind of blessing.

7

PHOTOGRAPHY WAS SUPPOSED to have saved me. It was supposed to have made me into something; made me look like whoever and whatever was behind my skin. After my mother's death, I stared at the wall where she had hung framed images of me. All fucking strangers—from cot to those final years in college. I had blond hair when I was a kid. Blond hair that Lily curled with her fingers before she took the picture. I had a beautiful face. I could be anything I wanted.

There were pictures of my father on that wall as well. Lily maintained she liked realistic photography. As things are, she said. In the butcher shop, where grains of bloodied sawdust clung to her shoes, where my father sliced into meat and posed as she ordered. 'Knife Above Flesh', she titled one. She said she could go professional if she wanted.

She photographed babies, Communion boys and girls and shopfronts. She photographed old farmers living alone who were lonely for women and gave me sweets. She bought books on photography. They grew in pillars in the sitting-room until Tom built shelves to suit them. He did everything she demanded.

Tom's face suited photography. It filled the lens with its thick flesh. It sponged up the light. Lily pinned his face next to mine and I know it frightened her when she looked at us both. I still had blond hair and I was still beautiful but as I grew older she saw something she despised whenever she touched my face and then its photographed replica.

'You'll turn out like your father.'

And I knew I was supposed to say no. No, I was different. I was hers. We played games together and Daddy just never understood things. He cut up meat and wrapped it up for customers. He sometimes smiled when Lily took photographs but most of the time, he just stared as if he wanted to kill the camera.

I didn't want to be Tom.

I wanted to be whatever she saw when she was happy with me. I wanted to be as she photographed others. They had good faces. They opened their eyes and smiled. I tried that. I studied Lily's books and I acted out the faces in front of the mirror but even then I saw that something was changing inside me. Some poison lurked in my fingers and I began to hurt things. First the procession of dogs I had as pets, then boys at school—the ones with tender, vulnerable eyes and I used my fist to destroy that vulnerability.

Don't I look dead, Mammy? How the fuck was I supposed to know that? Lily said I was her beautiful boy. I was hers. No one else's. I was as she made me. She wanted me when she was dying and I kissed her goodbye as her fingers held onto me and her eyes tried to see mine. I held my breath so I couldn't smell her dying one.

When she died, Tom ripped her work into shreds and I let him. We stood like broken statues in front of the bonfire he built as it burned everything she had made, every photograph, every replica of us both curled up and died in that fire.

Neighbours said it was grief. They wanted to understand that madness of obliterating her memory and they assured my father she was in a happier place.

Neither one of us attended her Month's Mind mass. Lily was rotting in the dirt, Tom believed. Rotting where he couldn't be and when he was there too, he wouldn't feel her, there would be nothing left but just bones. Just fucking bones to cling to.

'What do you want?' said the blonde café waitress. She was pissed off since I hadn't looked at the menu yet. I was studying Karen's photographs instead.

'Coffee,' I said.

'What kind? Latte … Cappuccino … Mocha … Americano … Espresso … ?'

'The House kind,' I said. 'That means the common shit.'

'I know what that means,' she said. She walked back to the counter and gave in my order to the girl behind the coffee machine.

'I'd like something else,' I called out.

She started back. 'What?'

I looked at her. 'Are you busy?'

She made a show of examining the empty café, 'Run off my feet,' but she half-smiled back.

'Could you do something for me?'

'What?'

I pointed first to the photographs I took of Karen when she was asleep and then to the one where she stood in the middle of the room.

I tapped my index finger on a naked, sleeping Karen. 'Give me your opinion and tell me if that's art. You go to college?'

'Third year Med. student … Is she asleep?'

'No, she's posing.'

The waitress leaned down and her dyed blonde hair fell forwards against my ear. I smelled coffee from her mixed with the smell of the day's lunch. Her name badge said Daisy Farrell.

'What's that shadow?' she pointed.

'Me.'

A mug of coffee was plonked on the table by Daisy's workmate.

'Daisy, the floor needs doing.'

'Yeah. I'll get to it in a minute, Trish.'

Trish flounced off and Daisy sat opposite me. She wore too much mascara to go with the dyed hair.

'A doctor?' I said.

'Yeah?'

'So a naked body wouldn't disturb you.'

'Not a bit. They're usually dead. Either that or a rubber dummy.'

'Nice.'

'Yeah.' She smiled at me again before directing her attention back onto the photographs. It's a bit pornographic, isn't it? Is that the kind of photographer you are? I mean, don't get me wrong. I'm no Holy Molly. I think they're cool. They look great.'

'Thanks.'

After a few seconds she said: 'You pay people for this. For posing?'

'Never.'

'So I'd have to pay you?'

'Yeah.'

'Who have you photographed?'

I reeled off the names of people I wrote about, fucked and partied with. Daisy seemed impressed. She studied the photograph of Karen awake and staring into the lens.

'She doesn't look happy.'

'It's early morning. Not her best time and anyway I like realistic pictures.'

'That means no air-brushing then?'

'If you want it, you can have it.'

'She's really pretty.'

'She always is.'

'Cool. How much?'

I reached forward and took Karen's photo back. 'Depends on what you want. You have a boyfriend you want to thrill? Or just something for the mantlepiece?'

'How about both?'

'Whatever you want. I'm three hundred an hour.'

'Fuck off.'

'Or we could negotiate student rates. Think about it while you're mopping the floor.'

Daisy leaned on her folded arms and made a point of scrutinizing Karen's face.

'I want to look good,' she said. 'I want to look sexy.'

'Sure.'

'Nothing sleazy.'

'Fine.'

'What's the student rate?'

Daisy touched my hand. 'You've artistic fingers.'

'I know,' I said.

'I can give you fifty euro,' she stated.

Daisy lived in her parents' house on the Glann Road. She said they wouldn't be back from Galway for at least two hours and she ushered me into the sitting room. I acted busy and focused on a large plant in the corner.

'Don't bother,' said Daisy. 'It's nearly dead.' She handed me a coffee. 'A present from an ex. I just like to see it suffer. Once it's dead, I'll burn it. So where do you want me?'

All Daisy wanted—she got. Not a thing came off her body until I took them off as part payment. She seemed to expect that. She also expected me to know what I was doing. So I acted that as well ... during the photo session as well as the sex one. The whole thing was over in thirty minutes.

'Bit different,' said Daisy when we had another coffee.

'You're too used to students,' I said.

'I meant the photograph.'

'Yeah?'

'Yeah. Maybe I've just seen too many movies with photographers in them. I just thought you'd have more flair, that's all. Are you sure they'll look right?'

'Don't worry, Daisy. You'll look sensational, I promise.'

'Better than that girl?'

'A natural, Daisy. A fucking natural. Marilyn reincarnated with an edge.'

'Cool,' said Daisy.

After Daisy, I headed back to a pub. I got lost amongst the tourists and lined up my drinks in front of me on a table outside. I drank them one by one, waiting for the familiar sweetness to settle into me. I feel good when I'm drunk, Claire. Feel very fucking good. The more I drank, the more I forgot how I felt in Daisy's house where she had draped herself on the bed and smiled into the lens.

I didn't give a fuck about Daisy's eyes. They could have belonged to a doll for all I saw in them. Doctor Daisy and her too-sweet eyes and carefully arranged sexy bed-head hair with four buttons open in her blouse. Doctor Daisy with her very good body, which I didn't want to fuck. Doctor Daisy whose mouth tasted of coffee and tooth-paste and who checked the clock to make sure I was gone by seven. Doctor Daisy who made me realize I was fucking useless after all.

When I drank more I forgot about Doctor Daisy. I sat close to the window and watched it get very dark.

I made my way back to the house. Stood in the hallway and thought about finding Karen. Hey, let me tell you about the photo I never took. Let me tell you what it told me. Let me tell you about some kind of love.

Aoife's eyes came back to me and I tried to shut them out. They should have been in the camera, caught in the film that was never there. I stared at my face and said out loud, 'Buy some film, find someone else and do the same. Fucking easy. Easy as fucking.'

I went outside to the garden. There was still some sun left in the sky. I looked behind me and counted the patio steps that led up to the dining room. Walk back up there, I tempted myself. Find a drink, find a television—do something everybody else does. Eat, fuck and shit. Make it as simple as that.

I could have had Aoife's eyes.

I still held the camera. I looked back again towards the dining-room and I wanted Karen to come out through the doors and call my name. But nothing happened.

Instead I walked towards the oak tree and hid the camera in an empty terracotta pot. A narrow walkway ran from the oak to a small building at the far right-hand corner of the garden. Its door was unlocked so I walked in. The light inside hurt my eyes and I used my jacket cuff as a visor until I could see.

Preconceived notions get you every time. Expect an artistic domain and although it is laid out in front of you, it still surprises. I couldn't see Medb but I saw her work. It hung from the walls and it lay accordion-like against tables and shelves. It was strung out along washing-lines but I was aware only of its blinding and absolute colour.

I walked farther in and managed to swerve a path round a large table and a few stools, large and small. There were three old armchairs, one covered in blankets, and there were dirty cups, plates, paints, crayons, chalk, paper and the smell of someone at work. I turned to the drawings on the table and feasted on what I saw.

If it was pornography, well and good. If it was supposed to be something else, I would have fallen for that as well. What I saw made my heart slow down and my dick rise up. Medb had drawn people, who because of the shadows and light she had used seemed real. Women whose breasts hung with age and still suckled men, short-legged men with large hands spread wide on their own chests and their eyes looking out at whoever looked at them. There was nothing young and clean about these charcoal figures.

They hooked their legs about each other and their flesh stretched or folded with age and disease. Faces in rictus of sex, faces of death. A woman's breast peeled open to reveal a human-faced heart. Not her face. Something near demonic complete with fear and terrible joy.

There were penises that were puny and real. There were fucking couples who couldn't look at each other. There were skull-sketches with half-drawn mouths and hints of eyeballs.

She had also drawn individual hands with bone that shone through and clutched tassels of their own flesh. Hands that held cheeks or rubbed their thumbs across a solitary mouth. They cupped balls and a penis or they held a child's hand. They laid their fingers across the ribs of a male torso.

She had drawn fat also. Bulged into faces grotesque with sex smiles, thighs that reached nowhere but outwards and adult hands podgy with overgrown flesh.

I lifted each sketch close to my face and I heard my own breath hit the paper.

'Enjoying yourself?' said Medb's voice.

I held up the fucking couple sketch and said: 'Something tells me you never got a normal Valentine.'

She took it from me and studied it for a few seconds. I watched her face and it was like watching something that could not move. Her lips were pale and her hair was piled up but slipping. She wore a blouse I recognized and a smock open to the waistband of her skirt.

I wanted to yell, 'Boo!' like some fucking nasty from a fairy-tale.

I wanted to plunge two fingers inside her mouth and feel those pale lips break. I wanted to see her face fill with me.

Medb looked up and let the sketch fall to the table. 'If you wanted to see my work, you could have asked.'

I folded my jacket over my crotch and asked. 'Who buys it?'

'All kinds.'

I leaned against the table and smiled. 'You know, Medb, I'm all for the Marquis de Sade overtones but Jesus, this stuff actually sells?'

'It does.'

'I suppose you never can tell with the sickos in this world.' I swept my hand underneath the sketch pile, overturning some and revealing others.

'Are these real people or do you make them up?'

'Sit down, Noah.'

'Why?'

The thing that pissed me off was her face. Nothing moved. No emotion, no ticking of her eyes. I fucking hate the quiet ones, the ones that make you dig into them, make you work.

'Because you look like you might fall,' she said.

I nodded my head but I held onto the table's edge and I whispered: 'I'm joining the dots, Medb.' Her face still didn't change so I pantomimed each haphazard dot in the air. 'One: You invited me. Two: Your Dad wants me to tell his story. Three: The photograph. Four: No photographs of any of you except of Evelyn when she was a schoolgirl. Five: You drawing Karen. Six: Jarlath feels cheated out of his real life. Seven: It's interesting how your dad met your mum. Eight: I do have the balls because ... You need me, Medb, if you want to come out of this with an image that will sell.'

Medb's look mixed with the look she had given me in the pub. Not completely. Not exactly.

I put my fingers on her waistband. Her hands went out to steady herself and her breath hiccuped in her throat. I plucked her blouse free and placed my left hand inside it and onto her skin and for some seconds I only felt how soft she was until my whole hand rested there and then I felt ridges of raised skin.

I scraped my thumb over a short scar before it criss-crossed another, then another and my fingers picked out more along her breastbone.

My fingers traced along the edge of her bra, slipping from the cotton rim of it to the scarred skin beneath. I got hard and with the gush of its sensation came Claire's face as I dreamed of pushing her against her thirteenth-century Chinese cupboard; the memory of Karen when she first found me; the fucking hate that comes from nowhere and I did what I always did, just before I acted, just before I hit. I looked in Medb's eyes as I had looked into Karen's, expecting to see all the half-fear and expectation I could use, but Medb's face wasn't Karen's.

Medb's face looked young and clean. My left hand felt like stone and my hate pounded in my head. Fucking dig into her. Pretend she's Karen. Pretend she's Claire.

But Medb's scars were still under my hand. It wasn't Karen's body I was touching, it was Medb's and as I drew my fingers over each scar, I forgot Claire. I watched the blouse-covered hump of my hand travel over Medb's skin. I heard her breathing judder in her throat and although I didn't want to stop, the map of scars beneath my hand made me say: 'Jesus, Medb, what have you done to yourself?'

She withdrew and tucked in her blouse as she turned and walked towards the sink near the back of the room. She chose a glass from the draining board and filled it with water.

'I'll have one of those too,' I told her.

She filled another glass and placed it on a stool beside one of the armchairs and then she sat in the opposite one.

'Should I apologize?' I said.

Medb drank from her glass. I reached my armchair and sat down. I pressed my jacket sleeve across my face to mop the sweat. I tried to pull all I knew to the surface, all those little lies I could spin to make me take anyone and put them where I wanted, make me their saviour for as long as it suited, make me indispensable.

I could still feel her scars. I turned my hands upwards and the next thing I said had no real reason to be said.

'I could make something of you, Medb.'

She looked at me then and kept sipping her water.

'Is that what you want, Medb … Is that your motive?'

I switched my gaze from Medb to the pictures that hung on her walls. I opened my mouth to keep my questions going but the lurid, brilliant faces that stared down made my voice drizzle into nothing and right there in colour and glory was the last of William Belios' gifts in canvassed painted faces nailed to the wall. I recognized faces I had seen in the sketches, faces naked with their emotions; as if she had taken a knife and dug their expressions out of their skin; as if she had taken their hearts and moulded them into their faces.

I looked back at Medb. 'Did you draw Karen like that?'

Medb put down her glass. 'I drew her like herself.'

'Why did you draw her?'

Medb shrugged. 'Karen has an interesting face.'

'Would you draw me?'

Medb relaxed back into her chair and said, 'No.'

'You're lying.' I pointed to the large painted faces. 'If you can do that, you can do me.'

Medb looked up at her own work and my gaze followed the line of her throat down to her blouse's collar. There wasn't a mark on her skin above its rim. She smiled while she studied her paintings and said: 'I don't want to do you.'

'Why not?'

She directed her gaze back onto me, 'You don't have what I need, Noah.'

'Yes, I do.'

'I've read your letters, Noah, and I've read the books you've written. Do you think I'd allow you to put me into books like that?'

'Why not?'

Medb said nothing. I sat forward, dropped my hands between my knees and looked as harmless as I could manage. I studied her face and thought of her scars and I did what I always do, go for the red-raw nerve, the thing that's hidden, force it out and play its saviour. I tilted my head, counted to five and all the time she watched me. Hey Medb. Hey Medb. I cleared my throat and made my voice soft.

'I've seen self-harm shit before, Medb. It means someone's crying out for something. Some kind of magic word to make everything disappear. I can give you that. I can make you shine.

'I want to get inside William Belios and I'm getting there, Medb. All those dots, they're adding up. Look, Medb: you've read my books and you despised my letters but you invited me. You want me here. You need me here. Who do you want to be? "Daddy's Other Daughter" or "Medb Belios", who artistically went far beyond her father ...'

'You only want to be him,' said Medb.

Her voice silenced me. She stood up and walked over to her table where she began to tidy and section her work into neat piles. She turned sideways and looked at me:

'That's what you haven't got the balls for.'

Her cool accusation, her doll-bitch waist and the way she stood with her eyes set in challenge and inside my head were the images of her scars. Red-raw vulnerability and a fuck-off challenge.

'You made him into a god,' she accused. 'Wrote down everything in those letters of yours and hoped he'd kiss you better.'

When I reached her, her throat was high as she looked up into my face and her smile was easy as her words fucked me.

'You haven't the balls to be anything but him.'

I hit her. I hit her straight across her face and so hard that she fell in slow motion into a kneeling position. Her head flopped forwards and there was nothing but the sound of her low, laboured breathing until her hands moved, curled upwards as she raised her face to look at me.

'I can draw this,' she said.

She got to her feet and I stepped back. She held out her arms to balance herself then made her slow way to the sink where she found a cloth to wipe the blood on her face.

'I'm sorry,' I lied.

Medb patted the cloth along her upper lip. Blood dribbled from the corner of her mouth down her chin. I walked over to the sink, found another cloth and pressed it against the line of blood. My hand pulsated with the force I had used to hit her. I leaned back against the sink and I steered my gaze over her paintings:

'Is this the stuff Jarlath can't understand?'

She didn't answer so I reached out and took her hand. I turned it palm upwards to see the scars on her wrist. Her palm lay in mine and I felt my blood rush to my skull. I shut my eyes at the pain. I concentrated on the feel of her hand and my own began to shake. My guts twisted and I used my other hand to touch her healing scabs and old puckered scars.

I opened my eyes and saw her watching me.

'Medb,' I said. I wanted to look at her. I wanted to strip off the smock, unpluck the blouse from her skirt and before I'd get rid of that, I'd see her eyes and they'd make me go on until there was nothing but her and all the cuts she had slit into herself. All that I could touch and lay my face against because it seemed right, it seemed perfect and my face could fit.

I put my left hand on Medb to draw her close and I bent my head to her shoulder and thought if I stood a long time holding her, things would somehow make sense.

8

EVELYN NEVER got used to Africa. She was terrified of its age, of its heat, of its casual, brilliant violence that would spark from a minor, street disagreement and result in a man's chest carved open beside a rusting Pepsi-Cola sign. She was told such sights were normal and as a journalist she had to expect to see these things. In her notebook, she wrote exactly as she had been taught. The facts were always easier when on paper. It was only later when she had the time to think that the blood seemed real and the hatred absolute.

She wrote of how the heat crept into white people, infested them with a certain flavour of cruelty, sometimes so subtle it was barely more than how they dropped pennies into a waiter's palm at a hotel bar. Other times, it was murder although never really admitted to and never amounting to anything more than dinner-party rumours.

She wrote that the white wives were desperate to avoid 'going native'. All of them had a story to tell of someone who did. The loneliness explained it. It was a disease that made people remember that Africa was so very far away from their own homes and it demanded different rules.

'Everyone takes lovers,' a woman with very white freckled skin said to Evelyn. 'But we all keep to the same trough, don't we?'

Evelyn was known to sample. Seeing a man's chest peeled open and maggots threading their way into it, witnessing a young boy standing in the corner with his penis in a man's mouth, and diluting violence into reporter-speak did things to Evelyn. It made something inside her cave into nothing. It made her alone in a terrifying land and a stranger to herself, so much a stranger that she was afraid to visit home and when she did her accent had changed, had become English, and her skin was too dark and too dry. She was older and the high-ceilinged house she had grown up in threatened to smother her.

In Africa, Evelyn began to sample according to the stranger inside her. She began with what she knew: colleagues who drank with her, who popped peanuts in their mouths and hitched their barstools closer to hers. There was always the sweat in her mouth, in anyone else's, in her bed, on her limbs turned grimy from sex and the day's dirt.

By the time Evelyn met William Belios, she had grown into something starved of love, starved into something he could use.

I held Medb. I held her with my hand on her spine and her voice fed Evelyn's story into my ear.

It began with marriage to an ex-priest. It continued with a house in Mombasa, the former slave-trading city on the coast of Kenya and a large house with an enclosed courtyard in the Old Town section of the city.

William took his camera and left the house with his wife in it. He returned with photographed faces and Evelyn learned to live with them while her children learned to be quiet.

When her visitors turned up, they were surprised at the existence of a family.

'No pictures?' someone asked.

'We're shy,' said Medb and Aoife poked her from behind. Jarlath held his breath and Medb waited until she saw the skin beneath his eyes turn red before she dug her fingers into his mouth and made him breathe again.

The visitors laughed. Belios looked at Medb and she looked back. Evelyn wound her hand into the back of Medb's dress to anchor her daughter where she sat. Medb felt her mother's hand tremble. She looked sideways at the curve of her face and noticed how wide her smile was, like a smiley doll holding her fork in her other hand and not eating at all.

The visitors listened as William Belios explained why he photographed people and nothing else.

'It's what I see in them.'

'And what is that?'

'I see their suffering. And if I were still a priest, I'd see God in them.'

Michael Sullivan, Belios' agent, laughed before turning to Belios and announcing: 'The photography of William Belios is the image of humanity.' Sullivan spread his arms to gesture at the other visitors. 'All these young admirers of yours, Belios, they realize it.'

'Realize what, Michael?' Evelyn said.

'How brilliant your husband is, Evelyn.'

Evelyn raised her glass to her husband and then drank it clean. Her right hand screwed tighter into Medb's dress.

The acolytes desired some kind of salvation. They would sit in the chair William gave them, take the drink he'd offer and he would destroy them.

He was cunning. He was friendly and the acolyte would expect appreciation because who the hell else would come thousands of miles to a third-world country? Belios would be kind but the young acolyte was invariably a failure. A good amateur but only that. The faces he took had nothing behind the eyes. There was nothing real there. There was nothing that led to anywhere else. He reduced their fantasies to nothing but they would try to be brave and look Belios in the eye and say what Medb knew was in their hearts.

I will be you. I will be greater than you.

'You still writing?' Karen's voice broke through. I hadn't heard her come in. I twisted in the chair to look at her.

'Just a bit about their lives in Africa.'

'Yeah?' Karen reached up behind her neck and unzipped her dress.

'Yeah. Medb told me a couple of things ... so I wrote them down.'

Karen's dress fell to her waist. 'Did you fuck her?'

'No.'

'But you wanted to.'

'No.'

Karen shook the dress off her hips to her feet. She kicked it out of the way and caught me looking. 'What?'

'Nothing.'

'You don't look at me like that and see nothing, Noah.'

'Are you getting fat?'

'Would you fuck off?'

'Christ ... it's just a joke.'

'Do I look fat?'

'God, no.'

'You're sure?'

'Absolutely,' I said and went back to my work.

'Even when you're not looking you're sure?'

I looked. Karen had always been fanatical about her figure and I used to like it when I held her by the hips with my fingers buried into her concave flesh. Her skin was milk-white except for the bruises. I looked at her stomach and imagined it scored and slit just like Medb's. I could bury my face there.

'I don't see any fat, Karen.'

'I stink of sweat though. Another alarmingly wonderful day spent in Oughterard with one fucked-up boy for company. Jesus, I can't fucking wait to get back to Dublin. Bought mineral water while I was out. I don't trust the water here. Jarlath says it comes from the lake where farmers turf their dead animals in.'

'I'm trying to write, Karen.'

'What bit? Her bit? "Oh Noah, how we lived in Africa ..."'

'That's a shit accent, Karen.'

'Suits a shit story.'

Karen pulled on a dressing-gown and then dragged a chair close to mine. 'Have you any idea how fucked up these people are? You know what he does, don't you?'

'Belios?'

'No, Jarlath. Snorts cocaine like there's no tomorrow. Did it right there in front of me. There I am, admiring the mountains or the fucking heather sticking out of some bog, and out pops the cocaine—'

'Karen, I'm in the middle of things.'

'Then he offers me some …'

'Which you took …'

'Which I didn't take … and he said the weirdest fucking thing, said it gave him pictures in his head.'

'Well, he's always wanted to travel. He probably imagines the Taj Mahal or wrestling with some crocodile.' I glanced at her. 'Why are you so worked up? It's only a drug.'

'What did you do with her?'

'Nothing.'

'I was gone all day, wasn't I? Did you fuck her? I bet you fucked her.'

Karen grabbed my work. I didn't even try to prevent her. I put down my pen and waited as she read. She read fast then looked at me.

'What the fuck is this?'

'It's Medb's part of the story.'

'And that's important, is it?' Karen asked.

'If I want a bigger picture, yes.'

'Medb this. Medb that. Sounds more like a story she made up.'

'It's what she saw. It's important.'

'Well, I'm not surprised. Not the way you look at her.'

'For fuck's sake, Karen.'

'What?' Karen put a big, bright smile on her face and sat on the bed with her legs dangling in little-girl mode. 'I want you to love me, Noah.'

'Right now?'

'Right now.'

I crouched on the floor and crawled on my hands and knees. When I reached Karen, I kissed her knees. I kissed the inside of them and she shivered and I told myself it was easy. Imagine the cuts that should be where you are kissing. I growled and bit into Karen's thighs. She jumped and I imagined that Medb's newly healed scars opened beneath my teeth and tongue. I could hear her sigh. I could lie her back against the bed.

I dug my fingers into her waist, dug hard so she could feel me.

Her clothes were still on so I kissed her breasts through them. Join the dots, she had said. Her breathing slowed like a child falling asleep and I closed my eyes before I kissed her mouth. Everything was Medb. Everything. Her mouth opened into mine and she said: 'All this is better for the baby.'

I opened my eyes and saw Karen's instead. I couldn't move. The word 'baby' paralysed me. I looked at her smiling face and in slow motion I wondered if I had heard right. *All this is better, baby.* That's what she had said. But Karen kissed my face and said she didn't mind getting fat and anyway she had only been pregnant for a few months and nothing really showed. She hadn't wanted it at first. She thought if she didn't want it, then it wasn't real. She said it was weird, wasn't it—how babies creep inside you when you least want them? She thought I'd fucking freak. She had told Anita, who said if it wasn't going to be aborted then I had to be told.

And now I was.

Karen knelt on the bed and stuck her stomach out to show the curve.

'How long?' I said.

'Nearly three months.'

'Get rid of it.'

Karen placed her hands on her stomach. 'No.'

'Jesus Karen, you can't really want it.'

'How do you know?'

'Because of who we fucking are!' I watched her flinch and I threw her dressing gown over her head. 'Because of what we fucking do! Because you're a dancer! Because this was never on the fucking cards!'

Karen covered herself up. 'We'll have to change things, Noah.'

'We'll get that out of you. We'll do it as soon as I'm finished here.'

'I'm not having an abortion, Noah.'

'Jesus. Next thing you'll be telling me it's a sin.'

'We can do this, Noah.'

All I could think was that inside Karen was something I didn't want. A soft ball of growing flesh, maybe with my eyes. I thought of it like a parasite inside her, hooked inside her, making itself big and ready to come out.

'Things will have to change, Noah,' said Karen. 'It'll have to be different. I know it will be different but we can make it fun still and you actually love me, don't you? I mean, you have to love me, Noah.'

I said nothing but lay back on the bed and stared at the ceiling. Karen followed me and I watched her belly flatten out as she lay down beside me. I listened to her voice telling me how everything was going to be so good. It was going to be so real. We'd have normal birthdays, a child's birthday. A nursery ... a fucking beautiful one so full of beautiful toys but inside my head there was nothing but Lily's face and Lily's fucking belly and Tom the butcher-man with his tears, with his fucking God-on-the-cross gratitude for a miracle.

Karen began to kiss me again and slid her body on top of me. My mobile rang and before she could get rid of it, I snapped it from her hands.

'Noah ... Jerry here.'

Oh fuck, Jerry.

'Noah, I've bad news. Your father's in hospital and they're not telling me anything ...'

KAREN WANTED to come. I told her no. She said we could talk. About what? I said. About my father dying in some hospital and me expected to hold his hand? Or about the baby? Is that what she wanted to talk about? She said she was sorry. She nearly cried and said we could talk about anything.

'Your dad isn't going to die,' she said.

Karen and I were smoking on the front steps. It was half-four in the morning and a mist concealed the road, the river, and the whole goddamned village. My hands were shaking. My lips were dry. I felt like I was coming down. Karen noticed.

'Did you take your tablets?'

'I'm not going to freak out, Karen.'

'You'll need them, won't you?'

'Yeah.' I looked at her. 'I left them upstairs.'

'Okay.' She stamped her cigarette out on the steps and she walked back up and into the house.

I shook with the sharp dawn air. No one loves the morning. Any-body who says they do is lying. Mornings are dangerous. They spread out in front of you and you have to keep one step ahead. I've always managed that one. Always knew what to do, where to go and who to do. Never had a fucking problem.

I looked out towards the river and saw the mist was lifting. That fucking morning couldn't wait to announce itself. The front door opened and Aoife stepped out.

'Hi,' she said and sat down. She glanced at me, then back at the closed front door. 'Met Karen. She told me you're on your way to visit your dad.'

'He's in hospital.'

'Sorry.'

'He's probably dying.'

Aoife nodded towards the river and inhaled deep. 'Always hard to watch someone die.'

I sat down beside her. She smelt of stale bed and bad breath. She glanced at me as I looked at her.

'What?'

'Nothing,' I said.

'When can I see the photograph, Noah?'

I glanced over at the dawn-dim oak tree and I confessed, 'Forgot to put film in.'

Aoife half-laughed. 'Really?'

'That was a clever show, Aoife.'

Aoife fumbled inside her dressing-gown pocket and pulled out a few cigarettes. 'Want one?'

'Have my own, thanks.'

She lit one. I noticed her hair was down. It made her look young and vulnerable.

'I want to understand,' I said.

She stared at me. 'No, you don't.'

'Then why the show?' I said.

Aoife flicked ash over the steps. 'Do you love Karen?'

'I made her pregnant. I suppose that counts … And your baby?' I said into the silence.

'There was no place for it.' Aoife turned her gaze back to me. 'So I aborted it … You going to put all this in your book?'

'Aoife …'

'One of those "Tell-Alls" Medb says you're good at?'

'She said that?'

Aoife flashed a smile. 'What a pity she didn't do what I did. You could have made something out of that, couldn't you, Noah? You'd make her look exotic and sorrowful. She's not like Dad in some ways. She doesn't want to wait until she's dead before people think they know her.'

'Why?' I said and jerked my head back at the house.

Aoife stared into the brightening dark. 'One day when I was married, I looked into the mirror and no one was there. So I just came home.'

'And that's your excuse?'

'That's my reason. I just knew where I was safer, that's all.'

I thought of the old man dying in a wheelchair. I thought of him when he could walk. I thought of him fucking his daughter.

'Safe from what?' I said.

There was a noise of footsteps coming fast and hard. The door behind us opened up and Karen appeared, halted in surprise, looked at Aoife first, then at me. She had a plastic bag bunched between her hands, which she threw at me. Her sandals slapped as she walked down the steps and across the driveway to the car.

'I said you weren't coming,' I shouted.

'Tough,' she shouted back and stood at the passenger side, holding up the car keys.

'Shit.' I looked at Aoife. 'Fucking hormones,' I said. 'They'll be the fucking bane of my life … Safe from what?'

Aoife shrugged.

'Couldn't you love your husband?' I asked.

'He thought I was somebody completely different,' she answered.

Karen beeped the horn. I glanced over at her. She was just the same as always.

'When I get back,' I said to Aoife. 'I'll take another photo.'

'I'm sorry about your father,' she said and we both got to our feet.

'Thanks.'

I stepped down the last few steps and something she said made me turn to face her.

'What?' I asked.

'I said,' she repeated, 'I said: There comes a point when it's easier to let them go. You don't think it … but you wait for it.'

Karen beeped again and Aoife waved at her.

'I watched you on those steps,' Karen said.

I turned the ignition on and put the car in gear. 'And you watched me with Medb. Jealousy makes you ugly, Karen.'

'So you're punishing me? Anita said you'd do something like that. Like hell I'm going to be a single mother, Noah.'

'Then don't be a single mother, Karen.'

I was about to steer the car when she grabbed my hand and put it on her stomach.

'This is life inside me, Noah.'

'Oh shit.'

'We made it.'

'Give me my hand back, Karen.'

She let go. I sat back and watched as she put on her seat belt, then flipped down her mirror and checked her face. She saw me staring.

'What?'

I picked my words. 'You know, Karen, hauling a baby out of your cunt was never my idea of change.'

Karen's face closed in. We sat in silence until it just made more sense to drive the car out onto the road, out along the river and through the village. At the Galway side I handed her her portrait photograph.

'You look beautiful,' I said.

Karen stared down at it. 'I look old.'

'You look fine,' I said.

'I look old.'

Half an hour into more silence, my mobile rang.

'Hello, Noah.'

Jesus fucking Christ—Claire. 'Hi Claire.'

'Jerry rang me.'

'So?'

'I thought …'

'I'm driving, Claire.'

'Well you can ring me back.'

'The three months aren't up, Claire.'

'This is going to bring up things, Noah. I want you to know we can talk, if you like.'

'Oh God, yeah,' I said. 'I mean the fucking issues in me are only dying to come out, Claire. Fill a book. Fill a fucking book. Hey Claire, I'm grand. I'm ready to let go. Gone through all the stages in double-quick time. See the old prick there in the bed, kiss him once, kiss him twice, open the coffin and fuck him in.'

I switched off the mobile and threw it over my shoulder into the back seat. I clamped the steering wheel hard because my hands shook. I went cold but my mouth filled with warm water from my stomach.

I veered the car to the side of the road, stopped, opened the door and vomited out. Thin yellow bile greased the ground. I retched a few times more and inched my body back into my seat. The retching made my head thump. I rested it on the steering-wheel but I couldn't focus and I almost laughed despite myself.

Go blind on the way to Cork. No time like the present for a fucking epiphany.

I wiped my mouth and then checked my face in the mirror. I looked normal. My eyes looked normal. God-made eyes. I used my index finger to rub at my teeth before I put the car in gear and got back onto the road. Karen didn't touch me once.

We stopped for coffee somewhere. I went to the men's, took off my stinking shirt, washed my hands, armpits, dried myself with paper towels, put my shirt back on and only then did I dare to look at my face. It stared back.

Lily said I was beautiful. Lily said I had her inside. Lily said I was one of her two beautiful loves. Lily gave up when my face became Dad's. What's it like to see your dead face in a coffin, Noah? What's it like to stand before that bonfire with him beside you and know Lily's dead and is never coming back?

What's it like, Noah, to know you're fucking lost?

Lily's face behind the camera and I could see her smiling mouth. Do as I do. Smile like me. Come on, who likes a grumpy puss? Come on ... smile just like Mammy wants you to. When did it happen? When did it click in? Belios watched his mother fuck a Bolivian photographer and knew. When did I know?

When did I know I was lost?

I leaned in towards the mirror all the better to see the thick puffed skin under my eyes. I saw the open pores on the bridge of my nose, on my chin, the red shattered veins on my cheeks. I wanted to piss but I looked at my hair. There was not much dark left. I pressed it down, tried to flatten it behind my ears, shook it free. My skull shook too. I screwed my eyes against the pain, counted to ten and opened them up.

God-made eyes.

I was desperate to believe anything. A photograph is a photograph. An eye is an eye. Greying hair is greying hair. Hair dye is hair dye. Won't be the first, will never be the last. Everything will go back to normal. Make it up with Jerry. Scout out the latest wannabe, fuck them rigid if they want, make sure they get the glory.

I joined Karen, who was sitting under a café umbrella picking currants out of her scone while smoking. I ordered more coffee.

'Meant to give those up, aren't you?'

'You probably fucked her,' said Karen.

'We didn't fuck. We talked.'

'How bloody modern of you.'

'Yeah well, you're the ballerina. You only think in romantic terms.'

Karen raised her face to me. 'Why can't we have a baby? What's so horrible about us?'

'It just doesn't fit, Karen. Thanks,' I said to the waitress who brought out my coffee.

'It can fit us, Noah.'

'How?'

Karen cut her scone into three. Her face was tense and sad.

I stirred sugar into my coffee and said, 'What took you so long? When you went to get my pills?'

She shrugged. 'Couldn't find them at first. Then I rang Anita and told her about your dad.' She buttered the other slices and pasted jam onto them.

'Want to watch your appetite,' I warned.

She nodded, then shrugged again before biting into her scone.

'I thought you looked really good in the photograph,' I said.

She nodded again.

'What do you think, Karen?'

'Am I supposed to look some other way?'

'No. You're supposed to look like yourself. You've an interesting face.'

'What's that supposed to mean?'

I shrugged. 'It's arresting,' I said.

Karen dropped her scone and took out the photograph. She stared at it, then flicked it onto the table between us.

'I told you ... I look old.'

I remembered the faces Belios chose. I remembered how their eyes and skin sucked Belios' lens into themselves, right into their rotting and suffering fear of themselves. I remembered Aoife and I knew I had failed, but desperate fuck that I am, I smiled and handed Karen the photograph and said with a smile: 'Not exactly on his level, am I?'

Karen glanced at the photo again and put it back into her bag. 'Well, you're not a photographer, are you?'

'What if I wanted to be?'

'And give up what you're good at? Jesus, Noah ... don't get me wrong but that's just like what I'd get in those automatic photo-booths you see outside supermarkets. It's me, isn't it? Just like a pass-port picture.'

I drank my coffee in silence until she said, 'We can fit it all in, Noah.'

'Yeah?'

'Yeah. We take it day by day. We get used to things. That's what all couples do.'

IT TOOK William Belios quite some time to tear Evelyn apart. He learned all he could of her. He learned about her home in Oughterard. He learned about her school, her parents, her desertion of God and then he went deeper and asked her things he assumed she would long to tell, all the things to make her pretty in his eyes. That's how it was done.

Then he asked her other things. He asked her about the moments in other men's beds and watched how the fear coloured her eyes greener. He asked, 'When you are there, Evelyn, and all there is round you is the sound of the room, the sound of some man's breathing, the sound of yours, what's inside you then?'

Belios was clever. He knew that if he held Evelyn close she would choose to trust him. She would believe him when he told her: 'People who step aside from the rules are always more enticing.'

That why you married her, William?

It's the easiest thing in the world to pretend to save someone, Noah. And it's the most gratifying. You see … people are essentially desperate to smother their loneliness.

William brought Evelyn to a large house in the Old Town part of Mombasa. Evelyn wasn't particularly impressed and walked from room to room, opening cupboards and expecting rats. William issued her with two servants, Miriam for the kitchen and Roberto for the garden. Both a mixture of Portuguese and leftover slave blood.

'William, this place is a fucking cavern.'

William turned from the window and said, 'It's perfect for us.'

Evelyn turned in the middle of the main room and the light caught her movement.

He might have photographed her there and then. He even made a play of it and raised his empty hands in parody of taking a photograph.

'Don't,' she said.

Belios mimed throwing away the camera. He walked about and checked the walls in a methodical manner, all the time gaining ground on Evelyn where she stood absolutely still. He saw how she tried not to watch him but instead she focused her gaze outwards through the large window, its balcony, and the sun outside, the very air soaked through with sounds from the streets beyond the wall.

She turned her face as Belios approached.

'If I had been braver,' she said. 'I don't think I would have married you.'

'If I had been braver,' she said. 'I'd have stuck to the one night stands and never loved you.'

My Evelyn, said Belios, was very beautiful in certain lights and sometimes she could hide successfully from me. She could hide those eyes now and again.

Like Medb?

Like Aoife.

9

TOM LAY IN A BED wired up with tubes. He looked dead already and I wasn't a bit surprised when the little nurse's aide gave me that certain 'he's almost dead' smile.

I dragged a chair over and sat down. I wanted to see some justice in it all: Tom in ICU. Tom about to die. Tom not knowing I was here and waiting for the fucking drama to begin. Karen came back from the toilet, bent over Tom's face and kissed it.

'What did the doctor say?'

'Get a chair and sit down,' I said.

'Don't joke, Noah.'

'I was being polite. What the doctor said was that Tom stopped eating some time ago and just kept drinking. He shut the door on anyone who tried to help and then some fine morning he slipped, fell halfway down the stairs and didn't kill himself, so after a while he dragged himself out the front door and someone found him soon enough.'

Tom's face had blown outwards with drugs and bruises. His hair was full white and thick and even his eyebrows had begun to fade. A machine pumped his heart and I told myself when he died, that was it. That was the end and that was all I had to wait for. The End. I could do that. I could sit in the chair, let the machines do their tricks until the doctors came with their careful faces and their usual words: He's actually brain-dead. The machines have done all they can. Tom's not here anymore. Time to sort out the coffin. Time to drop him down to Lily and wish them luck.

Karen had got a chair from a nurse and sat down close to me.

'I wanted him to know about us,' she whispered. 'Are you sure he can't hear? They say people in comas need to be talked to. We should have brought music in, shouldn't we?'

Hey Daddy, just you and me again. Pretend we're back in the kitchen, left with nothing but what Mammy forgot when she died. Everything was useless then. All her books, the cameras you bought with the fancy lenses and up-to-date buttons. You wanted her to stay, didn't you? Wanted her to be yours only. I understood that. I'm not going to bleat—fuck that for a game of soldiers—it's just that I don't think I ever loved you. I don't think I knew how to do it and Lily didn't teach me.

You in the butcher's shop, she with her camera and finally me sent away. We must have looked normal to some neighbours. We must have been just ordinary gossip after all. Must have dressed up well for Mass. Must have cut up all the right cuts of meat. Must have taken all the right pictures of all the right people. Must have done things like everyone else.

Tom at the breakfast table and his big face and beautiful hands, not knowing what way she'd turn, humming just under his breath to keep his fear contained. Poor fucker, you loved her too much, didn't you? All dressed up neat at the breakfast table. All fingernails scrubbed clean of blood and the smell of meat masked by toothpaste. Sometimes just to be safe enough, you'd wink at me and say, Noah, boy, isn't your mother only wonderful with her Sunday breakfasts? Isn't she? And expect my reply, all the fucking time humming and fucking intermittent winks driving the shit up inside me, all the red-fucking madness of it scalding my insides so I'd go cold outside and I'd vomit the fuck up, all over her best Sunday tablecloth and he'd grab my head and then she would come screaming in, What the fuck have you done to him?

And Tom could say nothing. He'd just pull hard into himself

while she screamed more and hit and punched his face until he had to punch her back, just the one to make her stop and then breakfast was eaten in silence.

'I love you more,' Lily said to me. 'I always wanted you,' she said.

Until I became exactly like him on the outside. Can't remember if I mentioned that to Claire; can't imagine she could find the perfect little pill—which reminded me to take some.

'Back in a minute,' I said to Karen.

'Get me a tea on your way back,' she said.

Outside the room, the nurses assumed I was looking for the doctor to answer all my questions. They smiled their wonderful, understanding smiles and pointed me to the hospital café. Got a coffee and sandwich and found a seat half-hidden by a plastic tree. Plucked the corn kernels from the sandwich and replaced them with tablets. Added in more, kept adding them, thought about it and then sprinkled the corn back in for extra colour, then ate fast, drank the coffee, remembered Karen, then decided to wait some more.

Take a while, I told myself. Sit back and appreciate the view.

The view filled with people that one day I might have photographed. I though of Daisy Wannabe Doctor and her clear smile trained right into my lens. Holy fuck, thought I had you there, didn't I, Daisy? Only I hadn't. Knew the minute I saw her face framed, knew it in my gut when I heard her say, 'I love having my photo taken.'

Photography was meant to save me. It was meant to have made me into something. I could have had my face, not a replica of Tom's. I should have dyed my hair, lost weight, drunk only wine and been someone even Karen could impress. That would have been me.

Hey Claire, figure that one out. Claire with your knees just so. Claire of my dreams. Told you about my dreams, Claire? How they fucked me over? How I fucked you just to keep you quiet? How I plugged you up so your words couldn't come out?

Noah, this is you. This is where you fit all the explanations. This is where we will make you all better. This is where we fix you up after you break down. This is where we say you're normal after all.

I wanted the rape to be perfect. I wanted it to have everything. The lighting, the movement—even the silence just before she'd try to scream, that would have been the perfect music score. I knew exactly how many steps it would take me to ram her against the thirteenth-century cupboard. See the lacquered figures jump at that. I'd concentrate on how she'd cry just to that point where I'd have to cover her mouth. I'd hitch her open. I'd fuck her good.

And with each fuck of my penis, I'd say, Well, this is it, Claire, this is fucking me fucking you. This is what I can live with. Faces never lie, Claire. Should have learned that one, Claire. Hate does it, Claire. Love too. Always shows itself. Always wanted it. Ever since I saw the old Kikuyu man's face and knew I wasn't real and he was.

Ever since I crept into Lily and Tom's bedroom with a camera to photograph their lumped-together bodies, creeping close to see the bruises on Lily's skin, like blown-up freckles and the threading scratches on both their bodies. Ever since I took their photograph and all I could see were their limbs and hear my own breath just as loud as the camera click.

Always wanted what I couldn't have, ever since Lily came home one day and flung a packet of developed prints onto the kitchen table just as I was finishing some homework. She said nothing but switched the kettle on and stood waiting for it to boil. She smoked and tapped one shoe against the kitchen press skirting-board. I was writing out a new sentence with a noun and adjective and a verb when Lily told me to hold out my hands and she poured the boiling water down.

That's it. Fuck over.

I RETURNED to Tom's bedside and sat back down.

'Where's my tea?' whispered Karen.

'Shit, I forgot. Sorry.'

She put her hand against my face.

Her face became lovely with her tenderness and she stroked my hair and kissed my cheek.

'I'll take care of you,' she promised. 'I even told Tom that.' She smiled. 'Never thought I'd stoop to praying again.'

Last night when I pressed my hand into Medb's back and felt the ribbon of her back, I wanted to crawl inside her, fill up the gaps in her spine so she would have me.

The door opened and the doctor walked in. Karen grabbed my hands, swivelled in her seat and for all the world looked just perfect. They told me a few things I needed to know. Obviously the first was that I needed to prepare myself for the worst. The next, Tom's heart was swollen and there was no real hope unless a transplant miraculously announced itself and finally, Tom had said he didn't want to be resuscitated.

'That's impossible,' said Karen. She glanced between me and the doctor. 'Isn't it? When did he say that? When?'

'We have to do a few tests. If there is no brain activity ...'

'Then we can switch things off,' I finished.

I looked at Tom's grey old face in the bed. 'Hardly recognize him,' I said aloud.

'You should have loved him more,' whispered Karen.

I turned to look at her and her clear child's eyes stared into mine and made me shut down. She put her arms about my neck and pulled my face close to hers.

'You should have loved him more,' she began to cry. 'You should have loved him more.'

I shoved her back into her chair and the doctor stepped forward, his hands raised to do something. I put my right hand on Karen's shoulder and she turned her sobbing face into it.

'The tests?' I reminded the doctor.

He stood there and didn't move. 'This can be an emotional time ...'

'I know,' I said and my mobile began to vibrate.

'That should be off,' ordered the doctor.

I brushed past him and into the corridor that led down towards the café. Jerry's name was flashing. I pressed the red button and it disappeared. He rang again. I pressed red again. I walked through the hospital café and out into a crowd of smokers. Jerry's name flashed up again and this time I answered.

'Noah ... how are you, Noah?'

'Okay.'

'How's your dad?'

'Almost dead.'

'Jesus.'

'Yeah.'

'This is a mad fucking deal, Noah ... if you want to talk ... want me to come down?'

'And do what?'

'Noah ...'

I cut him off and walked back to the wide hospital corridor and looked at the nurses in their perfect whites with their gentle smiles. I looked at the relatives of the other ICU patients and I remembered Lily didn't even make it here. One day into the doctor's with stomach pains and then the verdict of cancer. Cancer breeding cancer inside her. She lasted almost six weeks then died in her and Tom's bed while Tom clawed his heart out with grief and I stood looking at her just dead face and told myself that somewhere in the tissues beneath, in the fucking sinews that held her together, there had to be something left. She had to still live.

'Are you all right?' said a nurse.

I was slumped on the floor and I shook my head. Something hot and vicious was inside me. The nurse tried to help me but I pushed her away and my mobile spun onto the floor. It skidded to a halt under a chair and she picked it up.

'These aren't allowed.'

I switched off the mobile and she walked me back—a tiny, blonde woman with springy nurse shoes and a very calm voice. When I arrived at Tom's room, the doctor was waiting.

THEY ASSUMED Tom wanted the last rites and Karen thought that was a good idea so I let her deal with things. The priest came in and Karen actually knelt. I stared at the priest. The priest smiled as if he understood but Karen tugged me down.

Tom's hand was on my eye level. I stared at its long fingers and I could remember them when he seemed to fill his butcher shop with his voice and smile for his customers. The way he held my mother's waist between his two hands and I don't know why I did it, but I pressed my face onto his hand and left it there while the priest said his bit. I heard something lifting out of my throat and I realized I was crying.

Karen put her head close to my shoulder but I shrugged her back. The priest finished his routine and everyone waited until I stood up and gave the signalling nod to the doctor who switched off the machine and stopped Tom's blood from moving.

I put my hand on Tom's face. He was lukewarm and all his bigness was diluted to nothing.

I stroked along the inside of his hands, over the lines and the scars from his butcher knives. I thought of him in the house without her, walking through the rooms and just his own footsteps to hear. I thought of him not sitting where she used to sit, just so he could imagine her there.

You were supposed to do better, Noah.

Fuck the past, Karen had said. But I could still imagine him as I had left him. Everything of hers burnt to ashes in the back garden. All inside me now, he had said, gnawing at his memories of her, not having the guts to do away with himself, but letting each day kill him. If he was alive, maybe I could ask him, why all those years without her if you loved her so much?

I sat down because I didn't want to look at anything anymore but Karen eased my hands from my face and said, 'Don't worry. We'll get everything done.'

I let her do it all.

There were friends of his who seemed to remember him and they came to the removal: brought their flowers, their holy cards and fucking prayers.

A little old lady found me and weaselled her fingers into mine as her face looked up out of her little black funeral hat.

'Wasn't your father a beautiful man? He loved you,' she said and joined the queue for the viewing.

'Nice little old lady,' remarked Karen.

'Yeah.'

'Probably gave you sweets when you were young.'

'Probably.'

'You're in shock, Noah.'

'Am I, Karen?'

'It's just the sadness is too much, Noah. It happens to loads of people.'

She hung onto me and gazed at the onlookers. 'Not many people.'

'Step aside from the rules and people forget you,' I said.

'What?'

'Something Belios said.'

Karen turned me to face her. 'Your father is dead in a coffin and all you can think of is that measly little fucker ... Jesus, Noah!'

I backed down. 'Sorry. Must be the grief. I'm not thinking straight.'

'Forget about him.' She looked about. 'As soon as the removal is over, we'll get over to the B&B, get some sleep and just get through tomorrow.'

'I'm not going to the B&B. I'm going home to Tom's.'

'It's a fucking kip, Noah! We can't stay there.'

'You don't have to.'

'I'm not leaving you alone.'

'I won't do anything desperate, Karen. I didn't love him that much.'

'Noah ... sometimes you scare me.' She held out his rosary beads. 'Here. You either put them in or keep them.'

I took them and approached the coffin. Tom looked good. The bruising had been pasted over and the coffin silk was bunched about his face so it didn't look as swollen. I dribbled the beads into a pool just above Tom's folded hands. At Lily's funeral they had entwined the beads through her fingers. Classic holy stunt. Made her look good in the end.

I glanced up and saw the audience trying very hard not to watch the spectacle. The lights hurt my eyes and I decided I was too sober. I nodded to no one and got the hell out.

Karen followed me. 'Where do you think you're going?'

'The pub.'

Karen's shoes scraped on the pavement, then clicked hard as she came near.

'You are going to the church. You are going to sit in the front fucking pew and you are going to look as if you want to be there. He was your father. You go near any pub and we're finished.'

As soon as the words were out of her mouth, the fear slid into her eyes. She reached out to touch my wrist and she inched her way closer. She put her head against my upper arm just as the mourners left the morgue.

I sat in the front pew. I let the prayers roll away and watched the inane, insipid faces of the saints. Never what God made. Blue painted eyes and untouchable stone skin. Karen mumbled responses to the priest's incantations and I felt nothing.

Belios saw all this and felt power. Belios used it. Used those spouting prayers, the 'round and round the crucifix' rosary beads, used the so-called love handed to him on a plate and ended up riddled with cancer and without his wife.

I began to laugh. Karen nudged me but I kept on laughing. I slipped forward and my head hit the pew's rail but my laugh was still low enough to masquerade as sobs. Karen put her lips to my ear and said: 'Shut up. Shut up.'

I lifted my face to hers and she flinched. 'Will I tell you why I don't love you, Karen?'

The praying carried on. I hadn't raised my voice above a whisper but it was like I had cut out her heart and turned it upwards so she could see.

I kissed her hard and the shock moved through her and the crowd. She tore me off her and in a whisper she hissed out: 'I told him you weren't coming back. I told him he was a sad miserable prick and you were worth ten of him. I told him he could keep his exotic life and that you had decided to write about someone else. That's what I told him.'

I slumped back against the wooden seat. Karen spoke a little louder so others could hear and she explained I was in shock. I watched her dab a paper hankie across her lips and shake her head a little when some old man asked her something. 'I'll be fine,' she said. 'I'll be fine.'

The priest watched from the pulpit as Karen said: 'Noah, we have to go to the house now.'

I looked up at her determined face and I said: 'When I was sitting on the steps you were with Belios?'

'Yes.'

'When I was with Aoife?'

The priest followed us out. Karen attempted to apologize but I pulled her away and we walked over to the car. Neither one of us spoke until Karen parked the car outside Tom's house. She peered upwards through the driver's window.

'At long last—home.'

She undid her seat belt and said: 'Noah ...'

'You tried to sabotage me, Karen.'

'Oh for fuck's sake, Noah! Jesus ... don't act as if I destroyed you. I just told him a few home truths.'

'What did he say?'

'I'll tell you later when you're kinder to me.'

Karen waited for me by the front door. I could only make out her outline. I stumbled a little and she put out a hand to steady me. Her breath was on my face as she tried to kiss me but I twisted to put the key in the lock and the smell hit us.

'Jesus fucking Christ,' muttered Karen and waved her way into the kitchen. I followed her and threw the keys onto the kitchen table while Karen struggled with the back door, opened it and fanned air through.

'You could have looked after him better,' she accused.

Karen left the door open. 'Will I make coffee?' She rammed the kettle under the tap and said, 'Thank fuck for that,' when water sloshed into it. 'Where are we going to sleep?' she asked as she plugged it in and began to search for mugs.

I sat down and watched her. 'Wherever you like.'

She turned and put two mugs on the table. 'Not his room.'

'Fine.'

She opened the fridge and put milk on the table. 'Your room,' she said.

'Fine again,' I said.

'Get to see your Baby Boy room,' she smiled.

I smiled back then looked down at the keys on the table.

'Noah … ?'

'Yeah?'

'I'm sorry.'

'Really?' I spread out the keys into a steel fan and I could hear the fear in her voice.

I picked the keys up into my fist and it shook like an old man's until Karen drew the keys away, then placed her hand on mine and forced it down onto the table. My hand didn't stop shaking and the heel of Karen's hand ground into my knuckles as if by such force she could smother my trembling.

'Did you mean what you said in the church, Noah?'

I looked at her face and looked into her eyes and then I lied, 'No.'

'Then why did you say it?'

I pulled my hand from under hers, turned it palm upward and moved my fingers and she put her hand in mine. I kissed it then I kissed her and I said in a low voice, 'Sometimes I like to hurt you. You know that. The psychiatrist knows that but if I take enough pills, it will all fucking disappear.'

'I want this baby, Noah.'

I kissed her ear and mumbled something. She pulled away but touched my face. 'Babies are the most natural things in the world.'

'Your books tell you that?'

'No, my mother.'

'You've told your mother?'

'She's very happy for us … all right, it'll take her a little while to get used to the idea of us having kids …'

'Kids?'

'But she did say it was the most natural …'

'Karen … your mother says novenas just to get rid of me.'

'Yeah, well, that's not going to happen.'

'Kettle's boiled.'

Karen got up and made the coffee in silence. My hands were back to normal but I needed a fag. I also wanted to drink so I got up and walked into the sitting room. Karen followed me with the two mugs of coffee and stood in the middle of the filthy room, not knowing what to do.

'Noah ... what kind of life had he?'

I was over at the cheap glass cabinet Tom had bought a few years after Lily's death. There was an almost finished bottle of gin, dirty glasses, and an empty Christmas drink box I must have sent him once. I took the gin and held out my hand for the coffee. I drank a good bit then poured the gin into it, sloshed it round my teeth then swallowed hard. I shook my head and light zigzagged in my skull.

I revolved on my feet as I gazed about the room. The damp stains had caused the wallpaper to peel. The sofa was covered in old clothes, magazines, butcher paper and rotting food.

'Must be rats somewhere,' realized Karen. 'Noah, let's find a B&B.'

I don't think I saw Karen in the room. I didn't hear her voice. Instead I was standing in a strange room that I should have known, should have recognized as being part of me. I blinked at the doorway leading into it from the kitchen and I expected to catch sight of Lily moving from one room to the other, or maybe of Tom, or maybe just his voice reaching the back door before he did. I walked fast into the kitchen and shut the back door.

Karen ran to join me. 'You okay?'

I sat back down at the table. 'I'm fine.'

Karen sat at my side and said, 'Do you feel him?'

'Who?'

'Tom. Do you feel his spirit?'

'No, Karen, I don't.'

'Why aren't you talking to me?'

'Karen, what is it I am doing right now?'

'I mean ... you've had a great shock. They switched him off and you had to accept it. I mean if my parents died, I'd be in pieces. I couldn't live without them.'

'You've managed so far.'

'You know, when my mother saw a photograph of you she screamed and wouldn't speak to me for two days. She said she raised me for better things and certainly not to get involved with the likes of you. I rang her, by the way, and told her about Tom.'

'Did she say another novena?'

'She said she'd have a Mass said.'

'Nice. Pity you didn't keep the drawing Medb did of you. Her being the shit-hot illustrator she is. We could have had something there. Sold it to supplement the kid's education.'

I leaned my head back because I wanted the alcohol/coffee to reach every point of my brain. I wanted it to make me sleep. I thought of the faces Medb hung on her walls and their features distorted by what she found in them. I listened to Karen wash out her empty mug, unplug the kettle and tidy the milk from the table. In my mind's eye, I saw Karen's face hung on a wall but I couldn't see anything else. Just the child's face I had always known, whether under me, above me, at my right side, at my left side, in front of or behind ... I began to laugh and Karen told me to stop. I opened my eyes and she looked scared.

'Let's find that room of yours,' she said.

We climbed the stairs and I pointed out my room. She went in before me while I leaned in the doorway.

'How long since you've been back?' she whispered.

'Years.'

'It's empty.'

'Never the ideal childhood.'

'But there's nothing here but the furniture. Nothing of you.'

'Don't tell me: Mama's got your first tooth nailed to the wall.'

There were some old bookshelves left in the corner beside the bed and Karen trailed her fingers along them. She picked up a piece of paper, glanced at it, then dropped it.

'A receipt for something,' she said.

I just nodded.

'What posters had you on the walls?'

'None. I had photographs instead.'

She looked at me. Come on, Karen. Come on. Even you can see the connection now. Pictures on the wall. Boyhood dream screaming out at you. Me lying on the bed, doing worship, wanking myself so I felt good, so all the fuck inside me was quiet.

Instead of realizing all that, Karen decided to examine the bed. She ripped the sheets away and meandered out onto the landing to look for the hot press. She came back with a few sheets and a blanket.

'Surprised I found clean ones.'

'Tom always tried to be clean,' I said.

Karen dumped the sheets down onto the bed. 'Do you think we'll fit?'

'No problem.' I turned and walked across to the bathroom. Didn't look at anything, just took a piss and went back to Karen, who began to undress for my benefit. I sat on the bed as she hummed a little striptease.

I watched her dance and I thought how beautiful I could make her if I really tried. If I put Medb's body there, just put it where I could reach her scars and feel everything inside me go quiet.

'You look weird,' said Karen en pointe.

'I am weird,' I said and reached out my hand to her. She took it and fluttered down beside me.

When we were in bed, she wanted me to kiss her and I did. She wanted me to fuck her and I did that too. She wanted me on top and said it was kind of nice that way with the baby between us. She felt safe and wanted me to hold her that way for as long as I could so I turned her face to me and the late evening light from the window settled onto her eyes and made them look like glass.

'Hey,' I said. 'What did Belios say?'

She grunted a half-laugh. 'What?'

'You said you'd tell me later. This is later.'

Karen's glass eyes moved under me and I felt her breasts move with her deep breathing.

I kissed Karen's mouth and pressed my rib cage onto hers. Her breath came out in force and I said, 'I thought you wanted to be safe. I'm only trying to do what you want.' I put my hand between our stomachs and whispered: 'I wonder where it is now?'

'It's too early to feel him kicking,' breathed Karen.

I kissed her face and her hands and she grabbed my head and kiss/bit my mouth. I could feel her tears catch in the back of her throat and gargle her words as she blurted them out.

'He said he killed her.'

I lifted my face off hers. 'What?'

Karen shut her eyes for a few seconds then opened them. 'As calm as you please, Noah—he just said it out.'

I rolled off Karen and she sat up and scrabbled around for a cigarette.

'I was pissed off with you,' she said as she tugged a pillow from behind her and then sat up against the headboard with the pillow clamped against her body. I found my own cigarettes and sat up as well. 'I got your pills … I came out of our bedroom and I just wanted to go home. Instead I'm holed up in some house with the fucked-up children of some photographer who's never left the building.'

I reached for my empty mug and put it on the bed between us. Karen tapped her ash in and smiled her thanks.

'And curiosity got the better of me. So I decided to have a look at this guy who fascinates you so much. I went to his door and Aoife came out of it. She seemed a little surprised so it was handy to have your father dying as an excuse. I asked to go in and she said yes.'

'What was he doing?'

'He looked asleep. He was wrapped up on some kind of sofa-bed.'

'What did you do?'

'I looked around for a bit. All I saw were photographs and the odd weird little statue.'

'Your fingers are trembling,' I said.

'I didn't really expect him to wake up but he said hello and I told him who I was. I told him your dad was dying and I didn't think you'd be able to continue the interviews. I told him you had other priorities.'

'And what did he do?'

'He laughed. Then I thought he was choking so I went to the door and called for Aoife but no sign of her. He had stopped choking by the time I had got back and I could get this smell off him, like the sweet plastic smell you get from cheap sweets. It made me want to gag.'

'Then what?'

'He asked me to switch on the light next to him so he could see my face. He looks like he should be dead, Noah. He asked me what I thought about his work. I said I knew nothing about it but that you were going to write a book about him. Then he just laughed.'

'He laughed?'

'Yeah. I didn't expect that. Of course, he started choking again so I tried to pat his back. I could feel all his bones and his skin was shrivelled, like he was starving to death. I felt sorry for him. Jesus ... what a way to finish up.

'When he could breathe again he said you promised him a great deal and he knew you'd fail.'

Karen stopped talking and raised her eyebrows as she looked at me.

'Bullshit,' I said.

'Think what you want.' Karen lit another fag. 'Want to know what else he said? He said you wouldn't be able to write it down. Wouldn't be able to find the magic behind the words. He also said you wouldn't be able to resist exclamation marks.' Karen shrugged. 'I think that was his idea of a joke.' She pointed an index finger at me and added, 'I actually stood up for you. I told him exactly what I told you in the church and then he said he killed his wife ... just like that ... blurted it out ... So I got pissed off and I left ... and found you with Aoife.'

'Those were his words?' I asked.

'More or less.'

'And he said he killed her?'

'"I killed her." Definitely his words.'

I hit my head off the headboard and Karen's hand came up between it and the wood before I did it again.

'He's riddled with cancer,' soothed Karen. 'He's dying and dying people say some strange fucking things. It doesn't have to mean he actually did it. It doesn't have to be real, Noah.'

I tried to touch her but she flinched away. She held the pillow very tight and tucked its edges under her arms. She wiped at her eyes and shook her head a little and when she looked at me she had the best and brightest ballerina smile.

'Know what I think?' she said. 'I think we're fucked.'

I had dreams. The sort Claire said I would lose some day. The sort that had always sat in my skull, threatening to come out alive. Once I had told Claire that Karen should have been the best thing that had ever happened to me. Told Claire I should have been saved.

She repeated the usual line: 'You only save yourself.'

Fuck, Claire, want me to write it down? Make it my anthem. Hey Claire, what if I gave you another version? What if I told you that saving is for fools? Couldn't I tell you that story instead of mine?

It's what you can live with ... that's what makes you.

I woke up with my fist trying to punch the life out of Karen's stomach. She was screaming and her nails gouged into my hands and her teeth bit into my arms. She was screaming my name over and over and finally I heard her and lifted my hands away.

Two or three seconds of absolute silence and I saw Karen's wild and terrible face. I looked down at my hands as they uncurled from their fists and I looked at Karen's stomach, still almost flat but red from my punches.

Karen made a sound like an animal and dived for my face. I put out my arms but she was too quick and her fingers dug into the skin beneath my eyes while her knee went for my balls. She wasn't screaming words but her yells tore into my head.

I grappled with her just enough to keep her from my balls. I bent from the waist to protect my head and she beat her fists across my back. Her sobs made her sound like a beast in pain. I turned my head towards her stomach and I kept on trying to say something. I kept on trying to say sorry ... sorry ... sorry but she kept on beating me until she couldn't beat me anymore.

Then she said: 'Get out.'

I lay on the edge of the bed and couldn't move. She kicked me to make me move. 'Get out. Get out,' she said in a quiet, tired voice. She looked away from me when I looked at her.

'I'll stay downstairs,' I said.

She curled into a foetal position with her back towards me and dragged the sheet over her head. I took my clothes and went downstairs. I dressed half-crouched to protect myself from the pain and then I braced myself against the table. I glanced towards the sitting room and realized we had left the lights on. I moved like a cripple into the room and across to the drinks cabinet.

There was nothing left and I walked back into the kitchen. There was light coming from the early dawn outside and I shivered in the kitchen's cold. I walked over to the sink and turned on the hot water tap. I watched until the steam rose up from the sink and then I shoved one arm under the tap and kept it there until the pain drove arrows into my head, then the other arm, then back again and so on and a part of me barely saw the man at the sink who tried to burn out the redness in him and vomit out the fear.

When I woke up I was on the floor. The pain swooped through me as I raised my arms to see my hands curled and blistered. I sucked in air and shifted to my knees, then to my feet. I moved my left hand towards the still-running tap and the pain nailed me. I hooked my elbows in and against the sink to force myself to stand and when I thought I had enough strength, I turned the tap off with my thumbs.

I shuffled backwards to slump into a chair and I waited for Karen to wake up and find me. When she did, she stood at the doorway and said nothing for a long time. I looked sideways out through the kitchen window then down onto the floor because I couldn't look at her. She hadn't really stopped crying and she said: 'I think you're going crazy.'

I nodded and didn't say a thing. I heard her footsteps until I could see her feet stop directly beneath my gaze and I just couldn't look at her. I felt her hands move across my hair and onto the back of my neck and she moved that bit closer so that my head touched her stomach and I could smell her morning smell. Behind her dress, she was warm and soft and I felt something open inside my gut and I couldn't stop crying.

Karen bandaged me up as much as she could with the tea towels she found and afterwards I walked outside, into the back garden. I could smell breakfast from next door. A family washing-line shook while some kid whacked at it with a long stick. I couldn't remember the kid's face. I couldn't recognize anything about him. I heard their dog bark and it sounded happy. Must be a new family, I decided. I'll go next door. I'll introduce myself and I'll say ... hey how about having my house too? Here's my house. Put the dog in it, if you like. I smile right into their village faces and try to look as normal as possible.

Karen came out to join me. She undid a little of the tea towel to look at the skin beneath it.

'We have to find a doctor,' she said.

'No ... no doctor. I'll just buy a tub of Savlon and that'll do the trick.'

'You could be crippled if you don't do something. What if your hands heal into claws?'

'Well, I could always use my toes,' I said.

Karen stared straight ahead into Tom and Lily's garden while I watched the boy continue to whack the washing line.

'It could be gorgeous here,' said Karen.

'Maybe,' I said. I glanced away from the boy to Karen. 'What time is the funeral?'

She still didn't look at me but she said, 'Eleven o'clock.'

We went back into the kitchen and Karen prepared breakfast while I wandered from the sitting room, up the stairs, along the landing to my parents' bedroom. I opened the door and expected still to see them inside as I used to when I would creep in and watch their bodies move and moan in sleep. It took me a while to decide to photograph them and when I did, no half-measures—I went for their faces.

Either together or apart and I made sure their faces filled up the lens. I photographed the freckles beneath Lily's closed eyelids. I photographed Tom's heavy face. I used Lily's favourite camera since I believed it must be the best. It made hardly any noise. A sharp click that froze my heart with fear and delight and I almost wanted them to open their eyes. Especially Lily. I wanted to lay my head down on her pillow. Open your eyes. Open your eyes ... and if she opened them, I could see right into her—past the geometric colour guarding her pupils, right into the black, right into where she could see me.

I listened to her breaths and watched as her lips parted with each one. I lay on the bed and hooked up my knees so that they touched her stomach. Her hand lay between us and I touched it. It was soft and lax and then her fingers dipped and slid between mine and I fell asleep.

'What are you doing?' Karen asked as she walked into the room.

'Remembering.'

'Remembering what?'

'Lily and Tom.'

Karen walked over to the window overlooking the garden. 'How come they chose the back bedroom? I thought most parents liked the front.'

'Lily wanted to see the garden.'

Karen piano-tapped her fingers on the windowpane. 'The place needs Trojan work now.' She turned and said to my back, 'Breakfast's ready.'

She walked downstairs ahead of me and into the kitchen. The table was set and a pile of toast was waiting. We sat down on opposite sides of the table and began to eat.

Karen's eyes were red and her cheeks were very pale. She glanced at me with quick desperate smiles and so I had to say: 'How are you feeling?'

'A bit fragile,' she answered.

I shrugged. 'A funeral's a funeral.'

'That's not what I meant and you know it.' She chopped her toast into eight pieces and poured more tea.

'I didn't mean to do it.'

'It felt as if you did.'

'I think it was a nightmare gone out of control. I'm sorry, Karen.'

We ate in silence until she said, 'Tell me about Medb.'

There was a three-second pause until I managed to smile.

I put my elbows on the table in surrender. 'Fine ... what do you want to know about Medb?'

'How does she kiss?'

'I haven't done that.'

'How does she fuck?'

'I haven't a clue.'

'Well, you must have done something.'

'I held her.'

'Well, then ... how did she feel?'

'Small ... narrow. I could feel her ribs and ...'

'And what?'

'And her backbone. I ran my thumb down along it, felt every

piece of bone.'

'And what did she do?'

'She leaned into me.'

'Must have given you a hard-on.'

'Can't remember.'

'Remember feeling her though, don't you? I bet she was soft.'

'Yeah. In places.'

'Where?'

'Karen … this is shit.'

'Oh is it really? And here's me thinking we're having an intimate exchange about the time we spend apart. All the top couples do it this way, Noah.'

I watched Karen butter her third slice of toast and then shovel marmalade onto it before cutting the slice into eight and then just before she bit into one, she said in a friendly voice: 'Come on, Noah. How hard can it be for you to tell me a story about Medb?'

'What would you like to hear?'

'Fascinate me about her time in Africa.'

'What do you want me to say?'

'Just what she said.'

'The family lived in Mombasa's Old Town district. They had two servants. One was a boy called Roberto, and the girl was Miriam. The house they lived in had a wall surrounding it and it was close to the harbour. There were markets, prostitutes, nuns on walkabout, Muslims, Christians, animal worshippers, Buddhists—a regular melting pot.'

'This is what Medb remembers, right?' interjected Karen.

'Yes,' I said.

'What else?'

'She remembers the heat, the smell. She said she never forgot the smell.'

'Of what?'

'The smell of the town crowded with people. She said Irish people don't smell that way. She said she misses it. She said that's why she gardens; it sometimes helps her to smell it again.'

'Are you having me on?' said Karen.

'No.'

'Tell me something else, then.'

'I'll tell you something about Jarlath and how Medb saved his life.'

I was warming up. I was seeing everything in my mind's eye and inside me the little demon was sleeping. The kitchen was calm. My tea tasted good and although the burning feeling was still in my hands and arms, it was bearable as long as I breathed a certain way ... in slow, out fast and dive again into the slow inhale.

As I began the story, I held the image of my hand feeling the length of Medb's spine. I remembered the weight of her and the slow in and out of her breath where her lips almost touched my neck.

'Medb never forgot the moment when Jarlath hit upon the knack of pretending he was someplace else, far away from the house in Mombasa. She told me: "Jarlath was a bit of a dreamer. He gave the impression of being a mild epileptic. His eyes would just glaze over and that was it, he was gone into some dreamworld."

'Evelyn stood in front of the mirror in the front hallway and Medb said she remembered how her mother had looked that day. Evelyn's face was pink and she smiled to herself in the mirror. She had fixed her hair up and wore new earrings. Aoife asked her where they had come from.

'Their mother had gone out for the day and William was on safari somewhere. There wasn't any real warning that Jarlath was about to go into one of his little silent fits. Either they happened or they didn't. The reasons why they did happen had nothing to do with the weather or anything else.

'Evelyn shook her head just to make the earrings dance a little.

' "A present," she said.

' "From Daddy?" said Aoife.

' "They're not from Daddy," Jarlath said and then he held his breath as Evelyn turned from the mirror and made her way across the polished stone floor, raised her hand and hit her son hard enough to make blood spurt from his mouth.

'Medb looked sideways at Jarlath and saw him gulp in air then turn and walk fast down the hall towards the kitchen and the yard. Aoife ran after him. Medb stayed for only seconds after but long enough to see her mother straighten up, return to the mirror and fix her hair and earrings one last time before she walked out the door.

'Medb found Aoife kneeling next to Jarlath's body in the yard. His heels weren't moving and neither was his head. His eyes were wide open and stared at the sky. Medb dropped to her brother's side and tried to make him move. His face was whiter that she had ever seen, except for the blood still on his mouth. His face was cold like the skin on candles and Medb put a hand on his shirt just where his heart should be and felt nothing.

'Aoife called Roberto for help while Medb tried to get his heart beating. Medb put her ear above Jarlath's heart and willed it to come back to life. She even gave it its beat. Da ... dum. Da ... dum. Da ... dum. Aoife screamed for Miriam and Roberto while all the time Medb beat out the rhythm: Da ... dum. Da ... dum. Da ... dum. She rubbed her hand on his shirt, then tore it open and rubbed his skin. It was still as cold as candles. She couldn't cry but there was a horrifying fear crawling into her fingers, telling her that Jarlath was dead and wouldn't come back.

'Roberto came as quick as Miriam did and Roberto knew some first aid so he looped his arms around Medb's body to make her let go of her brother and then he pounded on Jarlath's chest until Jarlath moved.'

'So Roberto saved Jarlath, not Medb?'

'Half and half,' I said.

'What happened then?'

'He was put to bed and the doctor was called. He was fine. Miriam gave him some lemonade and Aoife and Medb sat at the bottom of his bed until he fell asleep.'

'How sweet.'

'Yeah.'

'And that's how you're going to write it?'

'More or less.'

'Why did she tell you that story?'

'I asked her to tell me something.'

Karen screwed the lid back on the marmalade jar: 'Real little hero, wasn't she?'

I leaned my head back and closed my eyes. I wanted to sleep but the burning in my hands rippled throughout my body and somewhere inside me was the bitter realization that Belios had got one over on me and had used the one thing close to me, as if he had physically turned her round to face me and made his words come from her mouth.

I killed my wife.

They never found 'him', Jarlath had said. I opened my eyes.

'Hey Karen,' I said.

'What?'

'Did you believe him?'

'Of course not.'

'I promise, Karen … another few days and that's it. We'll go home. I'll phone Jerry. You phone your mother and things will be perfect.'

'How perfect?'

'Fairy tale,' I promised.

That was it. She smiled back. It was easy, Belios had told me. You can always sniff out the ones to use; they're so honest when they think they have you.

Karen drove straight through Galway without stopping and pulled up in front of the Belios house late that afternoon. Neither of us moved but both of us glanced at the front door.

'Promise me something else,' said Karen.

'Anything.'

'Promise me you love me.'

I drew the lie right up into my eyes when I looked into her face and then I swallowed it back down so I could imagine it near my heart—just to make it that little bit more real, then I smiled like I thought I should and I said: 'I promise.'

Somehow I felt good.

Jarlath answered the door and we both followed him to the sitting room where Aoife was waiting, as was Medb, as was Michael Sullivan.

Michael Sullivan sat like an old homosexual in a big armchair—legs crossed and a glass of whiskey in his hand. He had a pink-lipped smile and Medb sat close to him, leaning forwards. Her knees switched away from him when Aoife said my name, yet she took her time in looking at me and when she did, she had the cool look of Belios, smooth and impassive—the doll-bitch from the first day. I wanted her to look at me as she had in the pub but her eyes skimmed mine. Karen tugged me over to a mini-sofa and made me sit down next to her.

'Your hands,' said Aoife.

'Damaged,' I said. 'Had an accident with a kettle.'

'Not much good,' said Sullivan from his chair. 'If you have plans to photograph the children.'

His words jarred against his prissy smile. I hadn't noticed before how much of a homo he was. I didn't like the way Medb sat so close to him. I didn't like the way her head was half-turned towards him only. I didn't like the way she ignored me.

Not like Aoife. Aoife manoeuvred a dinner-table chair in between Jarlath's chair and mine and sat down with her hands in her lap. First she closed them, then she opened them, and then she twisted them into her skirt.

'Hey Aoife,' I said. 'How's your dad?'

'He's fine,' she said.

I sat forward and said: 'This is nice. You know, when you are going through a bereavement—you usually need people round you.' I looked up at her face. 'Yeah, he's dead. We buried him this morning.'

I didn't like Aoife's face. It was gentle and sad and looked like it came from a famous painting. Take a picture of her now and you'd have something. There you go—not only did I kill my wife but also here is the photograph of my incestuous daughter. See how beautiful she can be? Don't you want her? Enlarge her, frame her, and make her yours.

Aoife would look good on a wall, clad in black with her red hair and just that look. Belios' Babe. Good fucking label.

'Why are you looking at Aoife?'

That was Medb's voice. I coughed and shifted forward to return Medb's stare with all my might.

'I'm just imagining her in the lens. She'll look really good.'

'Have you photographed much, Mr Gilmore?' said Sullivan.

'Every chance I get, Mr Sullivan.' I smiled at him. 'My mother was a photographer. I learned from her.'

'Have I heard of her?' he asked.

'Unfortunately she was unsung,' I said. 'She could have been famous but she preferred the amateur life.'

'I see,' he said.

'Actually you don't,' I said. Karen dug me in the ribs but I kept on going. 'Actually it boils down to fucking choices, doesn't it? Get married as she did or not and continue as she could have done. A different life is a consequence of a different choice. How about you, Michael? Take your choices of clients—Belios for instance. If you hadn't chosen him you wouldn't be here now, would you? Wouldn't have known the family, wouldn't have Medb now, wouldn't be sitting here in this beautiful room, trying to shut me out.'

'No one's trying to do that, Mr Gilmore.'

I jerked my glance at Medb. 'What has she promised you?'

'Fifteen per cent. It's all quite normal, I assure you.'

I turned my gaze on Medb. 'I told you what I could do,' I said.

'Michael knows us,' Jarlath said.

'Fuck Michael,' I said.

'Jesus, Noah,' whispered Karen.

'I can do everything for Medb,' I said.

'Noah … you're acting crazy again,' said Karen.

'Medb knows it,' I said.

Medb reached forwards for a cup and saucer on the coffee table. It was only then I noticed the whole table had been set with tea and cake and someone had poured that tea for me and they had also given me that cake. I ploughed my fingers into the slice and then stuffed the mush into my mouth; all the more to stuff up the shit that burned my throat.

'He's been through a lot,' I heard Karen explain. 'Tom's death has nearly ruined him.'

I listened to her words and I watched Medb's face. I wanted those exact words to reach her and turn her eyes the same way

Aoife's had turned beautiful with sadness, so beautiful that I could kneel before her and feel warm.

Karen was pulling at my shoulder and saying my name. Medb's face was in front of me. My knees were hurting as I rammed them hard into the floor because I didn't want to move, didn't want to leave Medb's knees, didn't want to be away from her and the red, scouring rage rose up inside my chest ...

Michael Sullivan moved fast and forced my head away from Medb's lap so that I vomited onto the floor.

10

KAREN TRIED to clean me up. Took my pills and flushed them down, Claire's medicine included. She filled the washbasin in our bathroom and dunked my head in and when I pulled my head up for the final time, I couldn't avoid who stared at me from the mirror. I could do nothing but stare at his face, at the rubber folds of skin, which sat like sponge calluses; at his smile, that turned his eyes into someone else's.

'You look like shit, Noah.'

Karen had undressed and inched her elbow into the bath water to check the temperature. I watched her through the mirror.

'I can't see myself, Karen.'

'Of course you can, Noah. You're in the fucking mirror.'

I turned and looked at her as she soaped her shoulders. Her bruises were fading into the normal colour of her skin, making her look just as delicate as she always did. Her hair was pinched up with clips and the hot water was turning her face pink. Any other time, it would have been normal for me to join her. Instead, I sat on the toilet with my bandaged arms resting on my knees.

'You'll have to pay for the damage,' Karen said. 'But knowing them, they'll insist on a new carpet. The bastards will want the best.'

I motioned at her stomach. 'How is it?'

'It's still alive.'

'Sorry about tonight,' I said.

Karen wrung then snapped out a wet facecloth. 'Sure you are.'

'I never fucked her, Karen. I swear it.'

Karen placed the facecloth over her face. 'No, you just mauled her in front of me.'

I glanced sideways at the mirror and caught the image of grey hair and my new profile. 'I'm changing,' I said.

'You're getting old looking,' said Karen. She put out one leg, angled it from the knee and expected me to watch, which I did. 'I told you what you could do about that.'

I got up from the toilet and made my way to the front of the mirror. It showed me from halfway up. I was fleshy. My arms stuck out before me and my shoulders had the pasty-white gleam of fat. My face sat on top, squat and no longer beautiful. A lump dived into other lumps. I pressed my stumps against my cheeks and watched the flesh stretch and roll as if I could discover what Lily saw but it didn't exist. It hadn't survived.

I turned and looked at Karen. Water slurped against the bath's edges as she twisted her body to look at me.

'What is it, Noah?'

I got down on my knees and kissed her. I kissed her as if I could love her. I kissed her for as real as I could make it and she kissed me back, kept kissing me and even as I pulled away, she dug her fingers into my face to hold me still.

Her face was beautiful and something like the photograph I took of her. In my mind's eye I could see the ball of new flesh inside her, feeding off her blood, plumping up its face to look more human.

Something of me rooted inside her.

Karen forced my face near to hers and she cried against it and I felt the red-burn of my hands reach my stomach, which twisted and formed into its own ball. My breath lurched out and my legs slid on the towel on the floor. Karen clutched at me and she thought I was crying. She thought the long hard sobs that came out of me meant something good.

I slammed my mummified arms against the bath's frame and in my head, my words glared up in neon colour and although I shut my eyes, the colour got brighter and bigger. Hey Claire. Hey Claire. Ever tell you about my dreams? Ever tell you what they make me do? You and the thirteenth-century cupboard. You and your back against its doors. The feel of you. How your flesh flattens wherever I touch it. How you stop crying. How I make you stop. Where my hands fit, thumb and fingers, and how they press so I can feel the bubbles of your breath underneath my mouth.

Karen's voice was shouting into my ear while her hands tried to hold my arms down on the bath's edge. She leaned her weight down and she kept saying my name. Noah. Noah.

Make me stop, I begged her. Make me stop.

I stopped and then there was just the sound of her body as she slid into a sitting position in the bath. The red-raw burn soaked up the weight of Karen on my arms. I smelled the soap she had used and the sweet jam cake she had eaten on her breath. I could hear her baby-soft croon but I dragged myself free, levered myself up and left her.

I went to find Medb and I found her with Michael Sullivan. He had his pink and white hands on her drawings and his pink and white smile showed yellow-cream teeth. In another world I might have liked Michael Sullivan; might have found some use for him.

He smiled when he saw me and held up one of her illustrations.

'Quite something, isn't she?' He rifled through the pile and spread out his chosen ones. He stood back to admire them. I looked round for Medb and found her watching me. I began to move towards her but Sullivan put out one hand and stopped me. His yellow-cream smile filled his face and lifted his cheeks like a Cheshire cat.

'Mr Gilmore,' he said. 'Let us have your considered opinion about Medb's work.'

'It's good,' I answered.

'But it could also be labelled as sick, wouldn't you say?'

I glanced over at Medb but she was studying a framed painting of hers and didn't look at me.

He gestured around him. 'All these drawings and paintings. Parade them in front of right-thinking people and what do you think will happen?'

'Well … you could only use your imagination on that one, Mr Sullivan.' I went to sidestep him but he pressed his body closer and said: 'I don't actually think she needs you, Mr Gilmore.'

I looked down at his face. The smile had gone and his gaze hardened up the rest of his face. There was movement from Medb as she put down her painting and picked up another.

'You see,' he continued, 'what exactly can you offer her? A co-starring role in her father's life? A couple of her own chapters? You see the calibre of her work … she's much more than him. Much more.'

'And you'd know?'

'I've known her all her life. Well … intermittently, of course. Mombasa was never just down the road. But whenever I did turn up, there she was with her damnably brilliant pencil—an extension of her eye. I could see it. I'm sure her mother could see it. William was never really interested. He had his photographs and they caused the right kind of stir. They would have caused more if he marketed them correctly but he insisted on being a recluse.'

He turned to glance at Medb. 'She'd never be happy like that.'

'I can make her famous,' I said.

Michael held his hands a few inches above my own. 'I've read your work. She's read your work. You deal with people who haven't the first clue about real life. All their achievements exist in their fantasies. They want the likes of you to make them look good. And you do. No doubt about that … is there, Medb? Ordinarily you'd do but Medb isn't ordinary and compared to her, you are nothing.'

I stepped back and kept my eyes down. I counted to five and then in slow motion I watched my mummy arms clamp the homofuck's head and wrench it sideways. He screamed as I dragged him across the floor and threw him outside.

I locked the door. Medb had remembered where she was.

'What's this game?' I said.

She glanced up then back down at her work. 'I should ask you that. You're the one acting out.'

I made my way over to the sink.

'Hey,' I said. 'Hey Medb.' I didn't turn but she said, 'What?'

'Could you turn on the tap please?' I said.

She came close then and turned the tap on. I just wanted to see her eyes. I wanted to see how she used them.

They were grey or green or maybe blue if she turned sideways but she looked straight at me and more than anything I wanted to see her life in her eyes, I wanted to see that goddamned suffering. Everything Belios put there. Everything Evelyn fostered. Everything Medb kept for her own … I opened my mouth and said: 'Love me.'

I knew enough about eyes to notice her pupils dilate.

Medb fixed my stump arms against her waist while she tucked grimy bandage remnants back into place. I pressed my face close to hers and whispered, 'Fuck me,' just above her ear. Her smile showed up in small lines about her eyes. I kissed her there. I opened my mouth so I could breathe her in.

I felt the bubbles of her breath as she pressed her face against my throat. She kissed my throat and she placed her hands on my stomach.

There was no sound from her except her breathing and I shifted my arms from her waist to her back. I couldn't feel her spine but her breasts pressed against me and when I looked down, I saw the open collar of her shirt and faint, silver scars. I shoved my mouth in close and suckled.

Her hands moved to my head and her fingers spread across my skull. I sucked in the pain when she touched the cut in my scalp.

I hitched her closer and then up. I kissed her mouth and she acted like a doll in my arms, stiff and staring. I stared back.

'Fuck me,' I begged. 'Love me,' I whispered.

Her eyes were grey now and she kissed my mouth. I walked her backward to the armchair and put her into it. I didn't have to beg. I watched as she undid her painter's apron, undid her blouse, the band of her skirt but she took nothing off. I came closer and she undid my shirt while my dummy arms brushed apart her blouse and I could see each scar, new and old, ready and waiting for me. Her doll-waist shivered when my bandages touched it.

'Hey Medb. Hey Medb,' I murmured.

Her hands lifted my head almost level to hers. 'Tell me what you can do,' she whispered.

'I can make you famous,' I told her.

She leaned her head back and studied my face. 'And what about my father?'

'He's old,' I said. 'He's dying. You're the one that's left.'

Medb reached for my grey hair and pushed it clear from my face. 'You'd forget him that easily?'

I didn't want her to talk and so I bit her flesh just above her bra and I felt the shudder from her cunt upwards. Her fingers forced their way into my mouth and I didn't let go. She moved forward in pain and slapped her hand against my mouth.

I looked up at her eyes and they glazed just like any other woman's eyes and I knew if I could have finger-fucked her now, she'd ram forward just like any other woman. I wanted her eyes to change colour. I wanted to look at them and see me as if I was inside her there, fucking her inside out—spine, blood, veins and flesh—filling her so that everything inside me was in her.

I rasped my tongue along the cuts in her thigh and I felt her shudder again.

I looked up at her eyes and said: 'Show me how you cut.'

That surprised her and wiped the glaze from her eyes. She took her hands from my head and gestured with one towards the press under the sink. I got to my feet, made my way to the sink and found a green tin box. I flipped open its lid and saw plasters, gauze, antiseptic ointment and razor blades in plastic. I closed the lid, walked back to Medb and handed the tin box to her.

She sat straighter in the chair, upturned the box in her lap and picked out the plasters, gauze and ointment and put them on the table beside her. She tore the plastic from the razor blades and chose one before placing the others on the table.

She looked at me. 'Where?'

I nodded at the waistband of her skirt and she stretched the skin tight above it. I shook my head and motioned further down. She rolled her waistband down and I nodded at the skin above her hipbone. She stretched her skin again and I watched her turn the blade against the rise of her hipbone. She turned it this way and that.

'Why are you stalling?' I said and my gut went cold, screwing its ball of shit tight. Medb didn't answer. Hey Medb. Hey Medb. She drew the blade from her hipbone downwards.

Inside my mummified arms, my hands curled and flexed and the pain thrilled me. My face flashed up in Medb's eyes; no glaze—just me and the colour of her eyes crowding round me and then her hands positioned my stumps either side of her waist and I held her as she slid to the ground.

My stumps held my body up as she undid my trousers and then rucked up her skirts. I was still in her eyes when she made me fuck her, still in her eyes I cried out her name, still in her eyes when I fucked out the images of Claire, then Karen, then nothing and then I realized the only sound was my own breathing.

Her eyes stared up at mine.

'Tell me you need me,' I said.

She said nothing.

'Tell me you need me,' I repeated.

She drew her arms up along my back and said nothing. I kissed her mouth and dug my tongue in to make her talk. I stopped when she didn't fight me. I raised my face and she touched it.

'If I loved you,' she said, 'how would you believe me?'

Medb dragged herself from underneath me. She fixed her bra and swept her skirt down. She put on her blouse and strapped her apron around her waist.

'I've work to do,' she said and walked over to the sink and filled a glass with tap water.

I put my shirt back on and I was almost dressed when she said.

'Michael Sullivan believes in me. He looks at my work and he sees what I want.'

'Which is?'

Medb turned her glass upside down on the draining board and jerked her head at the floor.

'Not that.'

'Then what is?'

Medb lifted her gaze towards her paintings on the wall. 'Those,' she said. 'And those,' she nodded at the stacked pile leaning against the armchair. 'Also those on the table,' she said.

'You made them up,' I said. 'They're just your sketches blown-up and coloured in. That's what has Michael Sullivan on heat?' I held out my arms and bowed from the waist. 'The Great Belios reborn with crayons.'

Medb crossed the room to a line of shelves and chose three glossy soft-backed books. My books. She held each book up, face forward then she flicked one open to its very back page to display the photograph of my face.

'That's why he wanted you,' she said. 'Not for any of the shit you've written. Oh ... I've read and reread these. My father's right ... all those exclamation points. How the hell do you make room for them?'

Medb tapped my photograph. 'You're a bit younger here but my father liked what he saw. "Medb," he said, "it's just like something you'd draw." ' She turned the photograph to look at it. 'I think he tried to imagine you someplace else. I think he fantasized if he was back in Africa, he would have liked to be found by you.'

'Instead of Stephen Banks?' I said.

Medb glanced at me then shut the book. She approached and handed me all three. I could smell our sex off her and I tried to touch her but the books she had balanced on my bandaged arms prevented anything extra. So I stood there useless and waiting.

'What else did he say when he saw my face?' I asked.

'He said it was too good for what you wrote.'

'Do you like it?'

'Not fully.'

I had to laugh and the books fell. I kicked them to one side and I was still laughing. I held one arm against my gut and looked around for a chair. I sat down and sat back into it and my glance swerved across the floor where we had had sex and our picture flashed across my eyes. That sobered me. I stopped laughing and jerked my head backward at the door.

'That little prick out there can give you what you want? Maybe you should read my shit again. Not one of them ever sued me.' I leaned my head back all the better to see her and held up my arms. 'If these were in better condition and I had my camera I'd take your picture, put it on the book's front cover and put your name in big bright letters. That's what you want, isn't it?'

Medb sat in the opposite armchair. She hadn't closed her blouse cuffs and they fell back to reveal the patchwork of scars above her wrist.

'We can use those too,' I said.

She turned her inside arm away from me.

'You think people are going to admire your work and not want a piece of you, Medb? You think they are not going to want reasons?' I gestured at the books on the floor. 'You're absolutely right. They're shit but look at the material. Who's going to remember a singer who prefers pumping up her breasts to singing? Or some fuckwit of a so-called actor who thinks he has enough brilliance to rival Shakespeare? In five years, if they are lucky, they'll be doing something else.'

I leaned forward and fastened Medb in my sights. I imagined her under me. I imagined her smiling. I imagined her hands on my face and her mouth kissing me.

'Why shouldn't the world know about you? You're not your father. You don't have any reason to hide.' I had leaned forward just to watch her eyes but her face kept getting in the way. Her face under me, her breath and the feel of her breast in my mouth. I shut my eyes, opened them. 'You need me, Medb, because I can give you exactly what you need.'

Medb buttoned each of her cuffs and sat forward. Her hands picked up a pencil and a sheet of paper and placed it on her knees. She fiddled the pencil between her fingers and her gaze skimmed along the floor before it looked at me.

'Look at me a different way,' I said. 'Look at me the way you did in the pub. Look at me that way now.'

There was silence while I watched her eyes and watched her frown. Then they cleared and I knew I was hardly breathing as I watched the frown disappear and that look, the same as before, coloured her eyes blue.

Medb's right hand held the pencil and moved along the paper as she spoke, looked down, looked up, looked at me, and the expression I wanted never left her eyes.

'Today everyone insists on being too sorry,' she said as she drew. 'They want answers for everything. They want excuses ... You set that up well, Noah. You make everyone good in the end, don't you?'

'But what if they aren't good? What if they aren't sorry? What if they turn round to you and say, This is me? How would you make all that believable, Noah?'

She had finished drawing.

'Not everything has to be put down on paper,' I said.

'But that's what he wants, Noah. He wants his confession guaranteed by you. He wants to be seen by you ... by everyone.'

Medb tucked her pencil into her apron pocket and then turned her sketch round so I could see.

'Is that me?' I said.

'Would you like it to be?' Medb asked.

It was a normal drawing. My big face and the pouches of slack skin beneath my eyes. She had put shade in to add to my age. I looked old. My eyelids had a heavy Chinese slant and although I tried to look past them and inside to where she had dotted in my eyes, I didn't recognize myself.

'It's good,' I said. I nodded my head and growled up some enthusiasm. 'It looks good. Not as finished as what you've on the wall but ... maybe it's me.'

Medb dangled the sketch in front of her gaze, 'I suppose you want something extraordinary.' She handed over the sketch and I rolled it up before sticking it into my inside jacket pocket.

'Miss Africa, do you?' I said.

'Enough to fill a book,' she answered.

'Do you miss your mother?'

I have to give credit to Medb; she didn't flinch, didn't even blanch or swallow. None of the typical reactions for my Medb—she merely stared back at me.

I sat forward and Medb shifted her knees sideways. I tried to look as harmless as possible, tried to look as if the image of her under me with her scarred thighs wasn't in my head. Instead I glanced across to where my books lay on the ground and I said: 'You're right about that shit. It's amazing how it sells. Any one of those people ...

they sat just like you and they told me their secrets because they all wanted something. You're no different, Medb. Neither is your father. So now that our fuck is over, why don't you tell me if your dad murdered your mom?'

'I wasn't there,' said Medb.

'Where were you then?'

'In the house, drawing.'

'Where in the house?'

'In my father's office.'

'And he wasn't there?'

'Not all the time.'

'Stop playing, Medb.'

Medb reached over to her side and began collecting odd pencils and paper. 'He was reading a magazine and then he finished reading it. Then he got up and left me alone in the room. I just continued drawing.'

'What happened then?'

Medb's fingers picked along the spines of books and magazines she found under the paper and pencils. Her face was still pale and her voice was calm.

'Tell me from your point of view,' I said. 'Imagine it's your story.'

'I was just drawing. Then I heard Aoife screaming. Then I ran out. I followed Aoife's screams and I found her and Jarlath with my father standing next to where my mother was sitting in a chair by her desk on the guest-house veranda. Her neck was back against the chair. I remember the big hand marks on it. She was dead.'

Medb stood up. She clutched pencils and paper in one hand.

'Shit,' I said. I stood up too. I reached out and touched her waist and trailed my fingers along her skirt's band. I kissed her calm, cool skin. I kissed her mouth and my right hand found her spine, dot to dot and in and out went her breath and I didn't have to look to make sure … but I felt her free hand come up between us, palm facing my chest then she pressed it forward so her fingertips touched me.

'I can make it all believable,' I promised.

BELIOS THE PRIEST believed in confession. He said the Act of Contrition suited all those people who didn't step sideways. He watched them in those little confession boxes and anticipation soared in his bones. He saw their faces in the plaited shadows of the confession-grill and knew the ones who longed to be saved. All dressed up in their snivelling repentance and desperate to be whole again, desperate to be loved.

Evelyn was like that.

Sometimes when he beat her, her blood sprayed the length of the bed and she'd crawl to a foetal position and when he'd return with water to wipe her face, she would confess that he was right; she had done things so bad that only he could love her. She went on for as long as he wanted to listen and he always rewarded her with a smile.

'It made sense to carry that sacrament over,' Belios said.

'Fucking hell, William,' I said. 'A psychiatrist would have a field day with you.'

He sidled his gaze from me to somewhere else. I was sweating again and my hands shook within their bandaged prison. I stared down at white strips now come undone from where Medb had tucked them in. The thought of Medb made my gut warm up.

'Rather a foolish thing to do,' said Belios. He was staring at my arms. 'All the way up to your elbows. How will you work now?'

I nodded at the dictaphone on the table between us.

'Why did you tell Karen that you killed your wife?' I said.

'Oh, that.' Belios withdrew back into his chair. 'Some little unknown person comes into your room at night and you just confess, Noah.'

'And it's true?'

'And it's very true.'

'And they all know?'

'And they all suspect.'

'Why admit it now?' I said.

Belios grimaced as he shifted his head against the wheelchair's headrest. He raised his eyebrows. 'Repentance?'

'No fucking way,' I said. 'Don't tell me that. Who the hell believes in that shit anymore?'

'Why can't I be sorry?' said Belios. 'Why can't I seek something good at the end of it all?'

I stood up and went in search of some whiskey and I used the lobster method to pour a glass and carried it back to the table.

'Water,' said Belios.

I repeated the whole movement and brought him water, which he slurped and spilled before setting down the glass. I sat back down, hunched forward and took a drink.

'You told me saving was for fools, William.'

'I told you the truth.' His breathing grated and spit dribbled from his mouth. His fingers pulled at the blanket on his knees but I refused to help him as he dragged the blanket up to wipe at his spit.

'Don't play games with me, Belios.'

Belios shook his head and the spit hung like extra teeth from his lips. His breath gurgled from his throat and his hand flexed outwards at the water. I got to my feet and pinched up the glass to his lips. His head was fragile and his scalp glowed pink beneath the white hair. There was a sick and sweet medicine smell from his breath and I whispered just loud enough to be heard above his loud sipping.

'Sorry you fucked your daughter now?'

Belios let the glass fall. Breath and water spurted from him and he tried to hide his face. I forced his hands down with my dummy arms and felt the bones flatten inside his skin. His breath hacked out in short gasps and his eyes tried to glance away from me, tried to hide, but I was stronger. I was going to live long after I put Belios in the ground.

'Come on, Belios. You tell me. Fucking your red-haired daughter. Spitting image of the wife so maybe you decided reincarnation was the perfect alibi?'

'I love my daughter, Noah.'

'That can't be love,' I said.

'Why not?'

'Why not?' I repeated. 'Why not?' The words were too powerful. They multiplied in my mouth and kept coming out.

'She loves me,' said Belios.

I shook my head.

Belios pulled himself forward. 'She loves me. You find that impossible to understand—you with your morals. What can you possibly recognize in the love between two people?'

'That's not love.'

'So you say.'

'It's against nature.'

'Hardly,' said Belios. 'It's just against the rules man made up.'

'You're crazy, Belios.'

Belios shook his head. 'Never once have I used that excuse. Why should I hide? If you wrote me down, Noah, unadorned with any romanticism, wrote down my story—Ireland, Africa and Ireland again—used whatever photographs that added to the story, how do you think I would be seen?'

'A fucked-up, dirty old man.'

'Well, if you used those words, I don't think it would succeed.'

'That's your repentance?' I whispered. 'Have sex with your daughter and be loved? What kind of sick shit is that? You expect me to write that?'

Belios' hand touched my face and my words slowed down. His eyes fixed on mine and his thumb drew a line from my mouth to the corner of my eye.

'Just like a parasite,' he said. Belios pressed his fingers to the side of my head and then pressed his mouth on mine. I felt the dry cracked skin of his lips and the uneven hiss of his breath and then he withdrew and collapsed back into his chair.

My hands were shaking. I flexed my fingers and the pain spurted into my upper arms. I glanced at my whiskey and I undid the bandages with my teeth. My arms shone ointment-white in front of me, curved from the elbow and finished in raw, blistered claws.

'That's some sight,' I said against the pain. I moved one claw and fixed it round my glass. The glass slid into my palm and I sucked down the pain and held the whiskey in my mouth for as long as I could before I swallowed.

I stared down into the glass-covered surface of the table and watched the dark shadow of my face move. 'Medb said you wanted me because of my photograph. So tell me, old man, what was it you saw?'

Belios smiled at my face and then jabbed one finger into the darkness behind me.

'Those photographs you worship, Noah—what are they supposed to be? Just something caught. Just a person in a moment and what do you do? You give them a story. You do what everyone does. I looked at a well-lit publicity shot of you at the back of your book. I looked at your smile and then I looked at your eyes and I made up a story about what I saw.'

'What did you see?'

Belios shrugged. 'A young man with greying hair. Your smile was forced and your eyes were empty. It didn't fit with the exclamation marks.'

Belios dabbed the blanket's edge along his mouth. He glanced down to tuck it about his waist and then he looked back at me. 'Then again, it's not much different to the way people are seen in photographs these days. Everyone wants to look happy. They want to fit in. They want to deny their secrets. Oh ... I don't mean the information you concoct with their blessing. I mean what they hide.'

He nodded at his gallery wall. 'Those moments when they aren't aware ... split seconds when they forget you are looking at them, when they are vulnerable and themselves. Oh, I could tell the ones that acted for the shillings but it was the ones that couldn't look or were afraid to—they were the ones I wanted and it was easy. I was white; they were black. I was the rich "Bwana" and they were nothing, either in my world or theirs. In the end, they all looked.'

'"Eyes of the soul", eh?' I quipped and forced my red claw around my whiskey glass but Belios was too quick. His hand came down on mine and I stared at its cancer-shrunk skin. Age-spots and sores clustered over his knuckles and the smell of his medicated breath made me retch.

'All I did was use what I saw, Noah. It's all anybody does.'

Without thinking I lifted my other hand to wipe at my mouth and I saw what it actually was. A red stump bubbled with blisters. I turned my palm to face me and stared into the ruby-red guts of fucking nothing.

'Exactly,' whispered Belios.

He removed his hand but I couldn't look at him. 'And if I could use my hands, Noah, what a photograph of you I would have.'

I placed my fists onto the table just to feel its coldness seethe through the hot burn of my skin.

'Write me like that, Noah, and maybe you'd be worth something in the end.'

I looked at him. 'Who saw you kill her?'

'No one, I believe.'

'Same as Katya Dressler?'

Belios smiled. 'Exactly.'

1 1

B IOGRAPHY THRIVES on anticipation ... the confession
medium of our times. I went to Claire. Thought that would kill
the dreams. Give me the medicine and the magic words. Give me the
fucking affirmations to keep the baddies away. When Tom's coffin
swung into action and into its grave, I wanted none of the new Amer-
icanized fake green grass hiding the clay, making things just so clean
for me. No, I wanted to be crucified with grief and I pulled out all
the stops.

I tried to remember some good times and when I couldn't, I
made them up and told Karen just to gauge the sadness in her face
and then I tried to match it. I told her I didn't know what to feel and
she still said it was shock. I stood at the side of the grave and watched
Tom's coffin bump and slide its way in. It sat snug and I dribbled clay
onto its brass cross. The priest finished up and shook my hand. Karen
mentioned sandwiches in the pub. Good for Karen. I handed the
gravediggers a bottle of whiskey each and I watched them shovel in
the clay.

When Lily died, I think I cried. When Tom died, there was nothing left ... just the picture of him in my face.

'You should have loved him more,' said Karen.

I looked at Karen, who was crying with ease, and that little old lady hooked her hand onto Karen's arm. That old biddy could bring her stories of Tom to her own grave.

Anticipation doesn't usually work at gravesides. It dies. So you look around and you get it somewhere else. Claire would say anticipation is a spur. Like envy and hate, it keeps you going. See that one's life? I fucking want it. Buy the book, see the movie, and if that doesn't work buy the drugs then. See the fucking mirage. See what I mean about anticipation? Fuels you in all the right places.

It needs to build slowly and with any biography, you never go for the jugular straightaway. You take your time. I stood at Tom's grave, didn't cry and played up to the image of being numb. I ate a sandwich in the pub and the little old lady hunted me down. She knew Tom in school, she said. They courted each other for over five years until Lily came along. He was a good man, she said.

'Good with his hands,' I said.

The little old lady wore a dark green velvet hat and a black mourning coat. She had thick jewelled fingers and a bracelet on her left wrist. She had very white hair and blue eyes trained on me. She raised her gin and tonic and said, 'Aren't you the image of him?'

I nodded across to Karen, who was flirting with the barman. She had braced her legs against the counter and was on her second drink. The barman's head was too fucking close and I could have moved but the little old lady tugged at my bandages.

She wanted to talk about Tom. Her used-up, powdered face shone with the fucking hunger. Hey Tom, what do you know—your girlfriend here never stopped loving you.

'He had such beautiful hands,' she said.

More gin and tonic for the old biddy. Her lipstick was bright red and it seeped into the cracks around her mouth. A fucking lush beneath it all. The barman nodded across to me and raised an eyebrow—can you deal with her? I nodded back and shrugged—couldn't give a fuck really. After an hour, the little old lady had forgotten who she had been speaking to and started talking to herself instead.

Something I never told Claire: after Lily took me to the doctor and said I had been playing with the hot tap and the doctor believed her, she bought me an ice cream and said I hadn't good hands anymore. Her face was nothing like it had been when she was asleep and gentle, when I had held her hand because it made me safe. She ate her own ice cream in silence and when she smiled at me, her eyes slid sideways. I gobbled my ice cream and I tried to say things to make her look at me. I tried to say sorry but that word never really came. She didn't look at me for some time and not being looked at does something to you. In the end, it makes you forgotten and it makes you useless.

LATE THAT NIGHT I crawled into bed with Karen and I knew she was awake. She lay at the edge of the bed, hitched up tight. I switched on the bedside lamp and lit a cigarette. I dropped it and ash sprinkled onto the sheet. I thumped my fist onto any red spark, then sucked the fag back into life.

'You're like an animal,' said Karen from her pillow.

'Sorry.' I was surprised at my voice. It sounded calm yet my hands were shaking and I had to anchor one elbow into my side to hold my notes steady.

'What are you doing?' said Karen.

'Reading.'

Stephen Bankes wrote like a sixties travel agent. Paragraphs of the technicolor blues of the Indian Ocean and the rainbow dashes of Mombasa natives and visitors. He described how white the whites were. How blue some blacks were, how brown, how mixed—Chinese, Arabic, Indian, African, Portuguese, English—and that brought Stephen Bankes into the Old Town section of Mombasa and to William Belios' house.

'Actually resembles a castle more than a house,' he wrote in cod-conversationalist style. Another one: 'Belios is not a particularly Irish name and perhaps owes more allegiance to thirteenth-century Norman-French invaders than to anything Irish.'

Karen turned onto her back and saw my arms. 'What happened to the bandages?'

'I took them off.'

'Why?'

'Couldn't do a damn thing with them on.'

'Why are you shaking so much?'

'Can't stop it, Karen.'

She reached to touch me. I yelled out and she backed off.

'What happened?'

'I was with Belios,' I said.

'Did he tell you what I told you?'

I shook my head.

'So you're going to stay?'

I nodded my head.

'Tell me something, Noah. Is it the baby you hate or the both of us together?'

'You should just go to sleep ... Karen.'

'A baby is for keeps, Noah. The baby needs us. Jesus ... I even found out the sex for you. That bitch of a nurse screwed up her mouth and said, "Don't you want it to be a surprise?" and I said, "It's enough of a fucking surprise already." It's a girl, Noah.'

I got off the bed and gathered my stuff.

'Where are you going?' Karen yelped.

'I'll sleep somewhere else,' I said.

Karen collapsed back onto the bed. I pulled my trousers on and she said: 'I'm leaving, Noah. I mean it.'

'Get some sleep, Karen.'

I went down to the sitting room and stretched out on the sofa. I tried to fall asleep but kept waking up to the cool, dark silence of the room. My arms were throbbing and I chain-smoked to cushion the pain and to get rid of the silence, I phoned Jerry at home.

'Jesus, Noah. It's half-three in the morning.'

'You said if I needed anything.'

Jerry yawned. 'Yeah. Yeah, I know. Let me sit down. How are you?'

'I'm bearing up.'

'Yeah, well ... funerals are tragic, you know. Really ram it all home, don't they?'

'Did you get my message?'

'What message ... oh yeah ... I got something. Didn't think you'd be ringing me again so soon.'

'You said anything.'

'Yeah, I know what I said. What do you want?'

'William Belios.'

'Never heard of him.'

'Sixties, seventies photographer. Long before digital age. Fucking brilliant portraits; a recluse in Ireland, has three kids, one who is about to be huge in the art world. There's a story about a strangled wife and no killer found and ... a few other things.'

'You fuck off on me, Noah, and you still expect to do business?'

'I had a breakdown.'

'Yeah, right.'

'I'm fine now.'

'Write whatever the fuck you want, Noah,' said Jerry and hung up.

I turned on the main light and spread my notes out on the table. I arranged them in chronological order at first and then I played with time.

I started off in the middle and used the idea of family life in Mombassa, William and his brood and the interruptions of visitors and Michael Sullivan. That didn't look so good. Who the fuck beats up a potential witness to a story?

I threw Stephen Bankes in as well. I wrote up the episode of Evelyn in front of her mirror. Stephen Bankes and Evelyn. Evelyn needed love so she fucked around. William knew. Wasn't that enough for murder?

Okay, start with the past: Mummy fucking a photographer against the garden wall and dead Katya Dressler.

Or start with now: start with mystery, plain and simple. Start with questions. Write it backwards and graft the answers in. Put in Medb. Make it Medb; show how the past just doesn't lie down dead. Fuck you, Medb. Fuck your cunt. Fuck what you see.

Seated at the table, I unrolled her sketch and I stared down at my face. She had me—big face and punched-up eyes. She drew me cut-price and cheap in the manner of any side-street artist. I looked flat and old. I looked like nothing.

If I blurred my vision I could see the younger version of myself courtesy of the books she had used to copy and exaggerate it from. I turned the drawing face forwards onto the table and began tearing it into strips from the right side to the left. That done, I halved each strip and then I jumbled it all up. I got up in search of drink and ground up pills into the whiskey. Drank one. Then two. Then three. I ruffled the strips of my paper face, turned over each one and then played jigsaw for a while.

I was good at it too. My face looked real in the end. Looked like me. Grey hair came alive with charcoal and white paper.

'She has that kind of eye,' said Michael Sullivan's voice behind me.

I looked up and he pointed at the door with the whiskey glass he held in his hand.

'You didn't hear me?' He pulled out a chair and sat down and his glance swung across the table before facing me. 'You're very drunk, Mr Gilmore.'

'Do my best work like this,' I said.

Sullivan's neck didn't look much the worse for wear. His friendliness surprised me. He nodded at my jigsaw.

'It's amazing how she uses what she sees, isn't it? A flick of the pencil and voila, there you are. It's up to you whether you like it or not. Do you like it, Mr Gilmore?'

'No.'

'Ah well, I could say the usual thing. You just don't want to see the true you. Who does?'

He mock-shivered as he smiled and reached for the whiskey bottle. He poured into his glass and added to mine.

'I must admit', he said before he drank, 'that I didn't expect you to be so passionate.' His eyes saw the packet of pills near my red file and his eyebrows went up in dramatic response.

He smiled. He nodded at the notes spread in front of him. 'Medb Belios. People will pay attention to such a name and she's far more gifted than he was.'

Sullivan lifted up an imaginary camera and clicked it. 'It was all there for the taking with him and it's easier to make things look exotic in black and white.'

I looked at Sullivan's pink mouth and I watched how hard his hands clutched his glass.

I joined dot to dot and said, 'Do you still love him?'

He smiled. 'Not anymore.'

'Because of what he did?'

'Because of what he's rumoured to have done,' Sullivan said. 'But now I have Medb, so to speak, and it's important that you and I have ground rules.'

'I'm just writing the book.'

'Which version?' asked Sullivan.

'Excuse me?'

'Mr Gilmore, you're not an innocent. William is an old man and suffers from an incurable hunger to be finally known. A deathbed confession written to be sold. With Medb, it has to be different. With Medb, it has to be the beginning of a life and who writes a biography at the starting-point?'

Sullivan waved his glass over the table. 'No doubt you have your structure, your plan, your themes all pencilled in, but he is a dying man, Mr Gilmore, and dying men are soon cancelled out.'

'That's not what I want,' I said.

Sullivan leaned in to study my jigsawed face. He stirred it apart and then smiled at me.

'Then she will choose me above you. Medb is like that. If you don't provide what she needs, then she forgets you.'

He sat back in his chair and fixed his tie.

'What about Aoife and Jarlath?' I said. 'Are they useful enough?'

Sullivan raised his hands. 'They're her family.'

'Belios invited me,' I said. 'It's his story.'

'He can be in her story, Mr Gilmore.'

I dragged the shredded sketch into one pile and tried not to look too hard at the notes in front of me and I tried to remember what order I had placed them in.

Sullivan patted my shoulder with more force than a pink-lipped homo should have and then he left the room.

I picked out my face from the pile, laid it out strip by half-strip and then I spat hard and kept up a rhythm of spit until I could mould it into a soft mush with my fists. It sat like a useless unbalanced ball of nothing and I felt dead inside. Even the little demon I was used to had shut up. I heard the silence of the room surround me and I counted to three, then five and then I re-counted until I could reach forward to stack my notes one on top of the other in no particular order.

I walked up the stairs and into our room. Karen's suitcase lay closed on the bed. Her handbag sat on top of it and her summer coat was draped over the pillows. I could smell her in the room. I dumped my stuff on the desk and made my way into the bathroom.

I switched on the shower, undressed and got in. The water made the pain more vicious. It hammered onto my skin and the more pain it gave me, the more real and alive I felt. I lowered my arms to my balls, tried to feel my penis and imagine that pain would make it hard.

Yet nothing happened. I slumped halfway down against the tiled wall and I laughed. You don't have what I need, Medb had said. Now I didn't even have a fuck inside me.

I stretched out and turned off the water. It drizzled to a stop and still I didn't move out of the shower. I let the water drip-dry off me until I began to shiver and then I crawled out. I moved towards the mirror and looked at myself.

I was older. Funny how a few days destroy what had been there at the beginning. If Jerry saw me, he would freak. If Claire saw me, she'd shut the door. If Tom had seen me, I don't think he would have recognized himself.

I wasn't beautiful anymore. I was nothing but an old face slammed into a skull. Belios was nothing but an old man disintegrating into his chair.

I rang Claire.

'How are you, Noah?'

'Perfecting the Sweetheart Method, Claire.'

'Noah, why don't you come in and see me?'

'Claire, tell me how I can be normal.'

'You are normal.'

'That's a lie, Claire.'

'Noah, we can have a telephone session, if you like. If you talk, then I can just listen.'

'I used to want to fuck you.'

'Well ... that's usually called Transference. It's normal. A client transfers his or her need for acceptance and love to the psychiatrist. Boiled down ... it means you see me as a good authority figure and you want to be safe and loved.'

'But it's all shit, isn't it, Claire?'

'It's actually the normal run of things, Noah.'

'Nothing human is alien, right Claire?'

'If you like.'

'What I'd like is to fuck you.'

Claire was silent for seconds and then she asked, 'Why?'

'What I'd like to do is rape you,' I said.

She coughed and I could hear her rings clink against the receiver.

'Is that normal?' I asked.

'It's not alien, Noah. It's just not acceptable behaviour.'

'So I need to be saved from it, don't I?'

'You need help, yes.'

'So you lied to me.'

'When did I lie to you, Noah?'

'You said I could save myself. You said I was normal.'

'You are being too literal, Noah.'

'I feel something inside me waiting to get out. Only it isn't waiting anymore.'

'How about this friend of yours? Have you told him what you're going through?'

'I haven't raped him instead, if that's what you mean.'

'Noah ...'

'He's isn't any good to me now.'

'I'll make an appointment for you, Noah ...'

'I'm going to be a father, Claire.'

'Oh. All the more reason to get better.'

'What if I can't do it, Claire?'

'Noah, you can do whatever you put your mind to.'

'I don't think I want to, Claire.'

'Noah, grief is a natural aspect of life but it can destroy all the scaffolding you use to make your life good and it's all normal. Come back to me. We'll work through this ...'

    I switched off the mobile.

1 2

THE KEY to biographies is love. Not a carnivorous, first-time-soul-mate kind of love since that is ultimately useless ... but a measured kind of love, one that steps back and grades the information. Knows what to leave in, what to leave out and if, like Claire, you believe everyone is normal, then the story feeds itself.

Belios didn't love Evelyn but he loved Aoife. Any way you look at it, that's a better meal than chronological dot to dots. It sucks the reader in. Incest and murder without the guilt and surviving on the necessary belief that it's all the better to live with.

Katya Dressler was twenty-two when she was murdered, Belios remembered. 'I can still remember her voice, not exactly in my head but as if she was close to me with the sharp thin clicking sound of her shoes across her bedroom floor. She was laughing as she spoke. I can hear her words but I would have to make them up for you now. It's just the thought of her words in my head.'

'Why did you kill her?'

'Because I could.'

I stared at the old man's hands and he raised the one that held his cigarette.

'It would be—nice—if I could give a far better explanation. If it was madness or anger … perhaps it was regret. I thought she would love me, as I needed. She didn't. A cut-price whore never holds anything in special reserve. I was just around. I was Friday night's fuck.'

'What was it like?'

Belios turned his eyes on me. I made mine stare back.

'Power,' said Belios. 'You feel life moving under your fingers.'

He inhaled slowly and I watched his throat shiver. He sighed out the smoke and said, 'Then I presumed I should repent it. I became a priest. I became bored. Then I met Evelyn.'

'How did you kill her?'

There was a prologue to that. Evelyn discovered The Blue Room restaurant soon after she and William arrived in Mombasa. Blue because of the frontage and the cold glossy blue of the painted cement walls. She liked the tinge of cold on her skin whenever she entered. Samosas, Indian chai or Pepsi-Cola, unrecognizable curries with the guts of some animal stirred into them, ice cream and mint tea.

Evelyn always chose a table towards the back of the restaurant. She would sit down and take off her flip-flops so that her feet could cool on the cement floor. She'd take off her hat, fold up her sunglasses, check her watch and study the plastic-covered menu.

The waiter brought her what she ordered and she met him smile for smile. She was meeting her lover here. She had new earrings and wore make-up from Nairobi.

She had been waiting half an hour when he finally arrived in a fashionable safari suit with a band of mock cheetah skin sown onto his hat.

He leaned down and kissed her. He smelled of cologne and his English accent cut into the sound of other conversations. He looked nervous when he noticed so many black people sitting so near. A few seemed to know Evelyn. He smiled at them because Evelyn did. He leaned in close to her and kissed her mouth. His lips pulled back when he tasted the samosa spice on her lipstick.

She must have laughed. She must have kissed him back. She must have shook her head so that her earrings jiggled. Maybe he laughed back and then took off his cheetah hat and lifted his arms out slightly to cool his armpits where the sweat had seeped down towards his breast pockets. Maybe he looked like he loved her and because of that she handed over the camera film.

'Why let her photograph you?'

Belios watched my dictaphone. 'I miss the tape recorder, you know.' He drew himself back into the wheelchair and said, 'When somebody is no longer useful, when they have forgotten their role, it is always interesting to see how they expect to survive outside it. I let her photograph me and I let her give it to Stephen Bankes. It was obvious she wanted to please him.'

'So you were jealous?'

'Is that what you call it?'

'It's what everybody calls it, William. Maybe you actually loved her.'

Belios looked over to his gallery wall and I followed his gaze.

'Maybe she frightened you in the end,' I said. 'Maybe she got to you.'

'She was useless at photography,' said Belios. 'Always adamant that there should be accountability in people's lives. She tried to write stories ... tried to see into the world. She seemed to think if she loved enough, then things would make sense. That's what she tried to hide from me.'

'Like Aoife.'

Belios hunched forward to light his cigarette and he pulled the ashtray into the blanket-dip between his knees. His spittle spat out as he breathed deep and then I realized he was attempting to laugh but his lungs wouldn't feed him enough air.

He raised his head and looked at me.

'You don't think I can love?'

'No,' I said.

He shrugged. 'When I killed Katya it was as if I had done something unimportant. Not very necessary at all but once it was done— then who can blame me? When I killed Evelyn ...'

'How?'

William had returned from the Zambezi River and was catching up on mail from Michael Sullivan. Medb entered the room with her notepad and drawing pencils. She went over to the window and said, 'Jarlath is throwing chicken eggs against the wall.'

William nodded and hardly turned from unrolling a magazine from its postage bind. He opened it up and saw his photograph as a centrepiece to an inane article by a Stephen Bankes.

'It was just a photograph, William. You said yourself she was useless at taking them.' I fished out the photograph from my pocket and stared at the young Belios, his hand held up to his eyes as if he was shielding them from the sun.

'You were watching her,' I said.

'Of course,' said Belios. He sat straighter, winced and tugged his blanket about his waist. I balanced my whiskey glass on its edge then rolled it in a half-circle and played for time so that my brain could work.

'You didn't want to let her go.'

'It's a curious truth, Noah, but no one likes to be someone's leavings.'

'So you killed her.'

There was half an hour of daylight left and he could have waited until the dark fell as it always did, straight down with no creeping from the horizon and cooling the ground before cooling the air. He could have made full use of her walking back in the near dark from the guest-house veranda to check on Miriam in the kitchen. He could have stayed in his office and opened up the rest of his mail.

Instead, he told Medb to stay where she was. She looked up at him then down at her drawing. He left the door open after him and went out into the courtyard. Nothing stopped him. Roberto was manoeuvring the grass-mower towards the back kitchen but he yelled something and Belios looked sideways and saw Jarlath flinging chicken eggs at the kitchen door. The slap and dash of yellow dribbled down to the concrete step.

Jarlath flashed his smile for Roberto and when he noticed his father, the smile faded into nothing and the customary dazed look filled his eyes. Roberto reached Jarlath and Belios kept walking towards the guest house.

He could hear Roberto call Miriam's name and she answered it. He also heard the swing of the back door and then Miriam's high voice and Roberto's growl got weaker as the door swung closed.

There was nothing left but sharp sunlight and the sound of his steps and when he looked ahead of him he could see her typing.

He didn't call her name as he stepped up onto the veranda. She glanced at him and then zinged the typewriter onto the next line. The jug of water by her left side wobbled as Belios bumped the desk when he reached and put his hands about her neck.

Her cry cut dead in her throat. Its force and strength bubbled beneath his fingers, like separate knots of veins straining to free themselves. The typewriter buzzed just enough to make him aware of her hands digging beneath his fists and so he squeezed tighter. Her feet rammed out her fear on the veranda floor and so he pushed all his strength into killing her right up to the point when her eyes seemed to crawl out of their sockets as if they at least could survive.

'How will you write that?' wondered Belios.

I poured more whiskey into my glass and gulped it in. I held it long enough to make my mouth burn. No need for exclamation points now. Just the plain confession of a dying man.

'As is,' I promised.

'I imagine seeing that in a paragraph in your book, Noah. I try to see my words. And it's not enough.'

His laughter spat out and turned into choking.

'Why isn't it enough?' I asked.

He raised one arm and his hand caught my shirt. His nails dug into me. 'Why isn't it enough?' I repeated. I fumbled for the oxygen mask and he shook his head. His throat reared back as he swallowed at the air. He still had strength in him. His hand balled up my shirt. His words were in my head so I did nothing to help him while his throat kept on fighting to drag air into his lungs.

KAREN SAT underneath the patio umbrella with a drink in one hand and a cigarette in the other. I sat opposite her and she lobbed over her pack.

'Nice picture,' I said.

She blew out smoke. 'Yeah well, the way I look at it the kid has to be prepared for disappointment in her life. Why the fuck should I be the model mom?'

'You want the kid.'

'With you. I want the kid with you.'

I sat back and said, 'Phoned Jerry last night.'

Karen jutted her chin to exhale as she looked behind me and I twisted to see Medb and Michael Sullivan walk across the garden.

'He looks a bit worse for wear,' said Karen.

I shrugged and twisted back. 'What's that you're drinking?'

'Gin, I think. What did Jerry have to say for himself?'

'He told me to write whatever I want.'

'Well that's what you always do, isn't it?'

Karen looked beyond me and into the garden. 'What about her? You think she'll let you go?'

'Karen ...'

'Or maybe you think it's love, Noah? You know I'm not blind. Never have been and I've never been "holier-than-thou", not where you're concerned. I know how many offside fucks you've had and what do you know about my life when I'm away from you? It's a natural thing to do in our business—only trouble is, I want it all to be different.'

I caught her before she could get up from her chair. She looked down and laid her other hand across my arm.

'Give up, Noah. I don't think I want to care anymore.'

She leaned in and kissed my cheek, took the cigarette pack and her scarf from her chair and checked her handbag for the keys.

'I'm driving home. You can look after yourself.'

I didn't call her back. I sat and finished my cigarette instead. I glanced upwards to Belios' window, then I glanced behind me to where Medb and Michael Sullivan had disappeared and then I rang Jerry.

I saw Aoife approach. She was drinking tea and she looked pale. I watched how her hands changed grip on her teacup as she sat down.

She smiled and I smiled back. She offered me a cigarette and I took it. Aoife had long narrow fingers and yet her hands were small. I sat back after she lit my cigarette and wondered how I should behave.

The thing is, things are always too bright during the day. You think differently and actions the night before take on an abnormal gleam. Even if they seemed real.

Aoife and her daddy. Dying daddy and dying love. Love is meant to save you after all.

'I've phoned the doctor,' said Aoife.

'Good,' I said.

Like I said before, the key to biographies is love. The measured kind of love that makes you decide how best to write the story. Biographies survive on keeping the structure believable and what you leave in has to make up for what you left out.

Otherwise the dots don't join up.

Ever make a promise? Ever do a deal? Ever expect God to reply?

You can watch a man choke and things will still seem normal. You listen to the door open behind you and watch his daughter enter and nothing is said even as she sits opposite you. You watch her face rather than his. It has all the pain and beauty you want yet she does not look at you.

The old man's breathing changes into frenzied wheezing and still nothing is said when his daughter picks up a cushion and places it over his face. You both watch her father's body curl and straighten with the force of his suffocation and because there is still some life left in him, you put your hand there also and you press so hard, you can feel his eyes pulse until there is nothing left.

And afterwards, when you look at his face, he seems peaceful as if he had welcomed what you did.

The epilogue ran its course: Aoife confessed. Jarlath disappeared somewhere. Medb became known.

At gallery openings of her work, I would watch as she'd prepare her face with the anticipation, fear and artistic manner she used to draw people in, each and every one of them anxious to wallow in the story of the newly manufactured Belios.

Maybe Claire would make something of it all. Maybe she'd discover some sick and reasonable answer for what I did.

And if I believed in confession, I'd go back to Claire and tell her that when I look in the mirror I just see the face I live with every day.

And that's what makes you.